THE WATER REMEMBERS

GENE SCOTT

Edited by
CHRISSY CUTTING

The Water Remembers
by
Gene Scott

The Water Remembers

CONTENTS

Also by Gene Scott   vii
Prologue: ix

1. The Poison Keeper   1
2. Evidence Like Water   7
3. What Sarah Saw   16
4. Networks Of Resistance   22
5. The Mound Awakens   45
6. Toxic Waters   61
7. The Prisoner's Recognition   78

ALSO BY GENE SCOTT

Jellybeaners (2017)

The Testers (2025)

Debra's Song (2025)

PROLOGUE:

The Fire Carrier (1819)

Birds quit singing on eastern paths. God pinched their throats shut.

Chief Tsali felt the absence punch his gut—something animal, instinctive, older than language. Air thickens before lightning splits oak. Water stills before the bass rise. Warning signs that pulse through Cherokee blood since before white men measured time.

The dogs quit barking. Then started that low howl that crawls up your spine.

Fifteen horses broke through the dawn fog, riders wearing federal blue, appearing like bruises against the morning. Metal clinked against leather. Horses blew steam through flared nostrils. Men stank of whiskey, gunpowder, and broken promises.

Children froze. Women's hands gripped their work. Elders straightened spines bent with grief, eyes holding every betrayal they'd survived.

Tsali stood at the village center, his face empty of emotion. The sacred mound rose behind him, belly-shaped, older than memory. Atop it stood the council house where eternal flame breathed. Cedar and pine crackled. The fire watched with patient hunger, alive with a purpose that existed before English words poisoned Cherokee soil.

"The Great White Father in Washington sends greetings to his Cherokee brothers." The captain dropped his words flat and heavy.

The interpreter—half-Cherokee with eyes that ducked Tsali's—translated with mechanical precision, each syllable burning his tongue like unripe persimmon.

Tsali caught the missing words. The places where truth died between languages.

The captain dismounted. His boots punched into soil that had fed Cherokee corn since before his grandfather's grandfather drew breath. He removed his hat with false ceremony, revealing close-cropped hair that matched dead winter grass. Sweat beaded his upper lip despite the mountain chill.

"General Jackson himself authorized me to speak with you." The name tensed every muscle in the gathering. Sharp Knife—the man who counted Indians as weeds in America's garden.

"The Catawba violated their agreements with the Great White Father," the captain said, eyes measuring cornfields like a man at a slave auction. "They raid settlements along the river, killing innocent families. The President demands Cherokee warriors demonstrate loyalty by helping suppress this rebellion."

His words hung in the air, thick as old blood.

The young interpreter leaned close to Tsali and whispered words not meant for translation, "The captain lies, Chief. Last night at their camp, I heard the truth. No hostile Catawba exist."

Old Tsola watched from the mound's base, arthritis twisting his fingers around a half-finished river cane basket. His eyes—cataract clouded but still sharp with eighty-two seasons of memory—tracked the captain's hands and noted where they lingered and what they coveted. As the sacred fire keeper, age had weakened his body but strengthened his spirit to read intentions no paper treaty could hide.

The captain spread a map on the wooden table. Ink-marked boundaries slashed across territories like a butcher carving meat from someone else's kill. His finger traced lines that ignored rivers, mountains, and graves that held Cherokee ancestors since before his kind knew this continent existed.

"We need all your fighting men," he demanded. "A large force will convince the Catawba to surrender without bloodshed."

Tsali locked eyes with Ukweti across the gathering. The old

midwife had caught enough babies and washed enough bodies to recognize death's approach—how it slides sideways, wears friendly faces, promises life while hiding blades. Her head shook slightly, warning without words.

The mountain beneath them shuddered—not in body but in that half-dream place where truth speaks to blood. For one heartbeat, the captain's blue uniform transformed into a charcoal suit, modern and crisp, his face aged but identical in its calculating hunger. The council house wavered, became a structure marked "Watershed Management" surrounded by destruction—trees ripped from earth, homes splintered beneath dark water reeking of chemicals no Cherokee language named.

A woman stood in this vision, copper skin and fierce eyes echoing his daughter's face, though she wore strange clothes and carried strange tools. Her hands clutched evidence of crimes against the land, and poison transformed her blood into something new.

The vision lasted one heartbeat. Tsali steadied himself, tastingthat future—metal and decay and blood and money mixed together—bitter on his tongue. The captain stood before him in federal blue, but now Tsali recognized the pattern unfolding: this betrayal would repeat tomorrow, next season, next century.

The council debated through night and into dawn, firelight revealing faces carved with impossible choices. Some argued for refusal—the Catawba story reeked of lies. Others urged compliance—perhaps loyalty would finally force Washington to honor treaties already signed in blood.

"If we refuse," one elder reasoned, voice rough as hickory bark, "they will label us hostile. If we comply and leave our homes undefended . . ."

He swallowed the consequence. Their silence acknowledged what waited in that void.

Morning brought resignation. One hundred and eighty-two men would ride with the captain, leaving thirty-seven older men with the women, children, and elders.

Those two days pulsed with preparation and dread. Women packed dried corn and venison, memorizing their husbands'faces through touch. Children clung to fathers' legs like ticks to summer deer.

Warriors sharpened knives and tested bowstrings, masking fears no one voiced.

Beyond Cherokee eyes, Georgia militia gathered on Rattlesnake Mountain's far side, homespun gray replacing federal blue. They wrapped torches in oilcloth against the rain that fell like the sky wept in warning. Their whispers rode on winds that smelled of coming blood.

On departure day, the chief's wife, Walela, stood with the other women, watching their husbands and sons ride southeast. Rain plastered her pitch-black hair against copper skin, mixing with tears no one could separate from heaven's weeping. Horses'hooves punched mud with sounds like distant war drums.

"They ride toward nothing," Ukweti murmured. "The Catawba villages exist only in lies."

Five days crawled past. Life in Nikwasi adjusted to the men's absence.

Women harvested early corn, fingers working as if nothing had changed. Children dug clay from riverbanks and shaped vessels to hold what might vanish. Elders prepared medicines for wounds they expected but not the ones that would come. The sacred fire burned under Old Tsola's care, his cough worsening with each night rain fell.

Dawn of the sixth day broke silent.

No bird called. No cricket chirped. No squirrel chattered. Even insects held their breath.

The village dogs started that bone-deep howling.

Militia emerged from the eastern mist through pathways meant to stay secret. Fifty-three men materialized like frost turning to ice, their captain—the same man who had worn federal blue days earlier—now dressed in Georgia homespun, rough as the betrayal itself.

"Surround the village," he ordered, voice stripped of pretense. "Let no one escape. Remember what the governor promised—this land belongs to Georgia now."

The first shot punched through Old Tsola's chest as he rose to defend the sacred fire. His body collapsed on the mound steps, blood soaking into stone that had witnessed a thousand years of ceremony.

The flame behind him flickered then strengthened, as though drinking his sacrifice.

The mountain recorded the exact sound a sacred fire keeper's blood makes hitting stone—how it hisses like wet wood, how it smells like iron and cedar mixed. The mountain stored this memory for the daughter of a daughter of a daughter who would need to recognize that sound when she heard it again, a hundred and thirty-seven years later, though the blood would flow from her own veins.

The militia dragged screaming women into forest shadows. They bayoneted children who ran toward the river. They shot elders standing in doorways. The valley filled with sounds that needed no language—the universal dialect of human cruelty.

Sixteen-year-old Tsini—Chief Tsali's daughter—watched her mother's rape and murder before the militia spotted her. Terror crystallized into action. She gathered twenty-six children and led them to a cave beneath the mound, a sanctuary grandmothers'stories had preserved through generations.

From this hiding place, they heard their world end—screams fading to whimpers, homes crackling in flames, militia members laughing as they divided captives and plunder. The cave air thickened with fear and sorrow and swallowed tears.

As militia ransacked the council house and set torches to sacred beams, Tsini broke ancient taboo. She slipped from hiding andentered the burning structure to save coals from the sacred fire. Smoke scoured her lungs. Flames reached for her skin with hungry tongues. She emerged clutching fire in a clay vessel, determination burning hotter than her melting flesh.

When the retention ponds fail in 1956, a child named Esther will dream of this moment without understanding why—will wake tasting smoke, feeling heat against her palms, and hearing whispers in a language she half-recalls. When Watershed Management comes in 2019, that dream will map the path to evidence that corporate men believe is permanently drowned.

As Tsini pressed the vessel to her chest, the mountain showed her what her father glimpsed—future devastation on these same slopes, another catastrophe engineered by men wearing different clothes but carrying equal hunger. She saw a woman standing in poisoned water, clutching evidence of crimes against the land. She knew, bone-deep, that this woman shared her blood—that her determination would flow through generations to this distant daughter.

"Remember," the mountain whispered, voice grinding stone against stone. "Remember and prepare them."

When Cherokee warriors returned seven days later from their manufactured mission, finding no hostile Catawba, they discovered an apocalypse.

Their community existed now as charred timber and unburied bodies. One hundred and seventy-eight dead. Forty-six women missing —stolen as "spoils."

Two thousand acres of land "cleared for settlement."

Chief Tsali found his daughter Tsini in the high valley where the few survivors had fled. He found something else—a clay pot containing coals from the sacred fire. His sixteen-year-old daughter had broken ancient taboo and entered the burning council house to rescue the fire that sustained the Cherokee spirit.

The fire existed, though differently. The people survived, though wounded beyond words. The land remained, though violated.

As Tsali held his daughter, they shared without speaking the visions the mountain had granted them. They understood then that they fought not just for today's survival but for tomorrow's memory—that their resistance must flow through bloodlines not yet born. What happened to them would happen again, in new forms with the same essence. The betrayal would come in different languages, with different weapons, but with the same intent.

And the resistance would need to match it, endurance for endurance.

This pattern—betrayal disguised as alliance, destruction masked as progress, theft presented as manifest destiny—would repeat across Cherokee territory with seasonal certainty. It would evolve but never transform. Homespun militia fatigues would become corporate suits. Torches would become legal documents. Bullets would become toxic waste. But the men who calculate "acceptable casualties" would stink the same across centuries.

One hundred and thirty-seven years later, another catastrophe will strike another community in these same mountains.

Another group of powerful men will calculate profit from disaster.

Another young woman will recognize the pattern repeated across generations.

Another fire will need to burn through the darkness.

Tsini cradled the clay pot against her body, burns weeping on her palms. She whispered to the living flame, "Remember for us. When they come again, remember."

Her blood wrote this prophecy first. The mountains, patient as stone, would remember what men with maps tried to erase. The rivers would carry stories in their current. The land would witness cycles of exploitation and resistance that ran deeper than any mine shaft could drill.

The mound where Old Tsola fell would stand through five more attempts to destroy it. The sacred fire would burn through forced marches, boarding schools, and termination policies, though hidden from those who would extinguish it. Memory wouldcontinue, grandmother to grandchild, a flame that refused to die by force, policy, or time.

This ain't history, child. This story lives in your blood.

This is how it begins. This is how it always begins.

With a broken promise.

With a calculated absence.

With the destruction of what cannot be replaced.

But also—with a fire that refuses to die.

And a mountain that remembers.

Chapter One

THE POISON KEEPER

The radiation badge on my belt turned from yellow to black as I waded deeper. Death has a color, after all.

Contaminated floodwater soaked my thighs, cold as mountain creeks in early spring but wrong in all the ways that matter. This water shouldn't be here. This water carries corporate signatures in its chemical stink—decisions made by men in boardrooms who've never set foot in Cherokee Valley except to calculate its worth in minerals. Men who'd never feel water carrying their own poison back to them.

My dosimeter screamed, the sound cutting through ruined lab walls like a wounded animal. Three more steps, and I'd need bone marrow transplants. Five more, and I'd sign my own death certificate. Some calculations are simple like that. Others—like how many lives make an "acceptable loss" for quarterly profits—take corporate degrees and moral rot to compute.

The strongbox gleamed beneath a collapsed section of wall, stainless steel winking through murky water like a promise. I reached for it, fingers stretching toward what Sarah died protecting. The water rippled around my movement, a petroleum rainbow shimmering across its surface. I can taste chromium burning the back of my throat. Cadmium coating my tongue with metallic sweetness. Cesium-137 from the experimental waste facility that wasn't supposed to exist on company property.

"Thirty seconds more exposure, and you'll need a bone marrow transplant," Jamie's voice crackled through my hazmat helmet's radio. "The retention pond breach released everything from the north facility. Move. Now."

I took another step, silt shifting beneath my boots. "Sarah died for what's in this box."

"And you'll join her if you stay." Static garbled his words, or maybe that was just fear. "The EPA's flying in. Let them retrieve it."

I laughed, a sound like creek water downstream from a mine tailings pile. The Environmental Protection Agency. Same federal officials who rubber-stamped Watershed Management's safety protocols. Who accepted obviously falsified water quality reports. Who looked the other way when our drinking water started tasting like metal three years ago. Same agency that dismissed Sarah's concerns as "lacking scientific basis."

"They'll lose it," I said, taking another step. "Or classify it. Or it'll mysteriously degrade during recovery."

The flood claimed twenty-six lives in twelve hours. Twenty-six neighbors. Twenty-six futures erased by corporate calculation. The official story had already crystallized on news channels—a natural disaster, unprecedented rainfall, an Act of God. Unavoidable tragedy, not corporate negligence with bodies attached.

But Sarah knew. She documented. And then she hid the evidence where only I would think to look.

Another step. The dosimeter's warning accelerated to a continuous shriek. The collapsed wall created a pocket of air around the strongbox —a small miracle in this scene of devastation. I knelt, floodwater rising to mid-thigh, and reached into the shadow of broken concrete. My gloved fingers closed around the handle.

"Got it."

"Move, Esther. Seismic reading shows the rest of that structure's about to go."

I turned, clutching the strongbox against my chest like a shield, and froze.

A wall of water—black as night, thick with debris—surged around the corner of what had once been Watershed Management's state-of-the-art research facility. The second retention pond just failed. Exactly as Sarah predicted in her final, unheeded warning.

I ran, boots slipping on unseen hazards beneath the toxic soup. The lab's remaining walls groaned under new pressure—steel reinforcements that should've withstood earthquakes now surrendering to deliberately weakened flood controls.

My escape route disappeared beneath six feet of contaminated water.

"The rise is cut off," Jamie shouted through static. "Northeast corner—maintenance tunnel. It's your only shot."

I pivoted, scanning for the access point. There—a rusted hatch half-submerged but still accessible. I splashed toward it, clutching the strongbox with one arm while using the other to wrench the corroded handle.

It didn't budge.

"It's locked," I panted, the roar of approaching water drowning my voice.

"Override code. Sarah's birthday."

Of course. Sarah worked in this facility for eight years before she started asking inconvenient questions. Before she started collecting evidence. Before her "accidental" exposure filled her lungs with fluid and her medical charts with lies.

I punched the six-digit code into the keypad. For a terrifying moment, nothing happened. Then the mechanism released with a pneumatic hiss. I wrenched the hatch open and slipped inside, pulling it closed behind me as the second wave hit.

The maintenance tunnel stretched ahead, dim emergency lights casting everything in blood-red shadows. I removed my hazmat suit and sealed it in a containment bag. The dosimeter fell silent. The damage was done. Whatever crawled through my bloodstream now would remain, replicating through cells, altering DNA, accelerating cellular death. The question wasn't if it would kill me, but when—and whether I could finish what Sarah started before it did.

The strongbox pulsed in my hands as if the evidence inside was alive, demanding release. Its combination lock—six tumblers requiring precise sequence—had kept its secrets safe through flood and radiation and corporate assassins.

I knew the combination. Sarah told me during our last phone call, the one that ended with a gurgling cough and silence.

"It's all there," she had whispered, voice already liquifying from the inside out. "The falsified inspections. The deliberately weakened retention walls. The toxic waste they're hiding. The earthquake modeling that shows exactly what will happen when the ponds fail. And the memo— Her words dissolved into wet, rasping coughs.

"What memo, Sarah?"

"Crowder. Authorizing it all. Calculating the cost of settlements against the profits. Twenty-six predicted casualties. 'Acceptable losses,' he called them."

Twenty-six lives. Exactly the number lost when the first retention pond failed two days ago. Not an estimate. A target.

The tunnel ended at a vertical shaft with metal rungs embedded in concrete. I slung the strongbox across my back using my belt and began to climb. Thirty feet up, my arms trembling with effort, I emerged into the pre-dawn darkness of what had once been Watershed Management's parking lot, now a scene of upended vehicles and floating debris.

Jamie waited in an airboat at the perimeter, his lean frame hunched over the controls, dark skin gleaming with sweat and rain. His eyes— always so calm, so reasonable—now held something I'd never seen there: raw fear.

"Did you get it?" he asked as I climbed aboard.

I patted the strongbox. "Everything Sarah died for."

"Let me see."

I hesitated, fingers resting on the combination lock. A lifetime of Cherokee teachings whispered caution. Knowledge is power, but it's also a danger. What this strongbox contained would threaten one of the most powerful corporations in the country.

And Jamie worked for Watershed Management's environmental compliance division.

"Not yet," I said, pulling the box closer. "First, we need to get someplace safe."

Jamie's expression darkened. "You don't trust me?"

"I trust you," I said carefully. "But what's in here could get people killed. Already has."

"We need to know what we're dealing with."

The airboat's engine idled, matching the thunder rolling across mountains that had witnessed centuries of exploitation. The same mountains where my ancestors hid from militia during the Trail of Tears. The same mountains that taught my grandmother how to read weather in pine cones and find water with forked sticks and predict disaster in the behavior of birds.

The birds went silent three days before the flood. Just like they did in 1819 when federal troops betrayed my ancestors. The pattern repeating, generation after generation.

I thought of my daughter, Lily, safe with my mother two hundred miles away. I imagined her copper hair catching sunlight, her small hands that already knew how to weave simple baskets, how to recognize healing plants, how to listen when mountains spoke. Seven years old, and she already carriedthe pattern in her blood—the knowledge that betrayal comes wrapped in progress, that resistance requires memory outlasting extraction.

"Ruth needs to see this first," I said.

My grandmother—bearer of tribal knowledge and retired environmental attorney—would understand what this evidence meant on multiple levels. How to protect it, who to trust with it, and how to use it to hold Watershed Management accountable,not just legally but morally.

Jamie studied my face, then nodded slowly. "We'll head to the reservation. But Esther," he gestured toward my radiation badge, now solidly black, "you need medical attention."

"Later." I clutched the strongbox tighter, feeling its weight like a sacred responsibility. "First, we make sure this survives."

The airboat roared to life, skimming across floodwater now illuminated by the first rays of morning sun. Behind us, the Watershed Management facility continued its slow collapse, toxic secrets seeping into groundwater that would carry them downstream to communities whose names didn't appear in company reports.

Ahead lay the reservation—five hundred acres of sovereign land that had survived centuries of attempted erasure. Land that remembers what humans choose to forget. Land where my grandmother keeps the old ways alive alongside legal precedents and scientific principles.

I ran my fingers over the strongbox. Inside lay the evidence that would either bring justice or make me the next target. Inside lay Sarah's legacy—proof that twenty-six deaths weren't accidental but calculated, predicted, and accepted as a cost of doing business.

The radiation in my bloodstream had its own mathematical certainty—cellular damage multiplying by the hour. A clock counting down.

But I wasn't raised to fear death. I was raised to fear leaving work unfinished. I was raised on stories of ancestors who carried fire through burning buildings, who preserved language through forced relocations, who remembered water's original channels through centuries of dams and diversions.

Lily flashed in my mind again. The way she looked at me during my last visit, her head tilted like she could see something inside me I couldn't yet recognize. "You got the mountain in you, Mama," she'd said, small fingers tracing the lines on my palm. "Mountain don't bend, don't break, don't forget."

I wouldn't forget either. I would carry this evidence like Tsini carried fire through flames. I would make sure what happened here wouldn't be washed away under "Acts of God" and "regrettable tragedies." I would ensure this pattern finally broke.

Some truths are worth dying for. My grandmother's people have known this for centuries.

Chapter Two

EVIDENCE LIKE WATER

The strongbox sat between us like a coffin—too small for a body but big enough for truth.

The reservation clinic smelled of sage and antiseptic, a combination that always made me think of borderlands—places where different worlds meet without quite merging. Dr. Mordi Blackfox examined my radiation readings with the steady calm of someone who had treated uranium miners and nuclear test site victims for forty years. His weathered hands, precise as a jeweler's, drew blood from my arm while his eyes—dark as obsidian behind wire-rimmed glasses—calculated survival odds he wouldn't share.

"Potassium iodide," he said, preparing an injection. "Chelation therapy next."

The strongbox waited on the examination table, still sealed. Its stainless steel surface had been decontaminated, but what lay inside remained untouched since Sarah locked it three weeks before her death.

"How bad?" I asked, though I already knew. I could feel it in my blood—something changing at the cellular level, radiation becoming part of my body's grammar.

Mordi's mouth tightened beneath his silver mustache. "Bad enough that we should be having this conversation in Asheville Medical Center rather than my clinic."

"Can't risk it. Watershed Management has people in every hospital within a hundred miles."

"They have people here, too," he reminded me, nodding toward the clinic window where Jamie paced in the waiting room, phone pressed to his ear.

"He saved my life," I said, but doubt crept in like floodwater finding new channels. Jamie's quick knowledge of escape routes. His immediate availability with an airboat. His insistence on seeing inside the strongbox.

"So did Sarah. Look what happened to her."

My grandmother entered without knocking, carrying her eighty-two years with the straight-backed dignity of a woman who had argued before the Supreme Court, testified before Congress, and taught her granddaughter how to listen when mountains spoke. Her silver hair was pulled back in a traditional bun, with turquoise earrings framing a face mapped with lines of wisdom and humor.

"The water's still rising," she announced, fingers working river cane strips into the beginnings of a basket. "They've evacuated three more communities downstream. Official death toll is thirty-seven now."

I closed my eyes. "Sarah said Watershed Management predicted twenty-six."

"Corporate predictions rarely underdeliver," Ruth said dryly. Her fingers wove the cane in patterns older than the English language. "When money meets water, money always miscalculates."

She nodded toward the strongbox. "Is that it?"

"Yes."

"Have you opened it?"

"Waiting for you."

Ruth placed her palm flat on the strongbox's surface, as if greeting it. "Sarah came to see me two days before she died. She couldn't breathe without coughing up blood, but she drove all the way to the reservation to tell me she was gathering evidence. Said it would show a pattern going back decades."

"What kind of pattern?" Mordi asked, disposing of the syringe that had delivered chelating agents into my bloodstream.

"The same pattern government pens wrote into our treaties with disappearing ink," Ruth said, her fingers never pausing in their weaving. "The same pattern mining companies carved into our mountains with dynamite and legal loopholes. The same pattern nuclear plants followed when they hired our men for the dirtiest jobs without protection."

Her eyes met mine. "The same pattern that killed your father."

I swallowed hard. Dad died when I was ten. Lung cancer after three years at Oak Ridge, handling materials no one told him would poison his cells. Another "acceptable loss" in America's nuclear ambitions.

I entered the combination—six numbers representing the date the Cherokee Nation signed the final removal treaty. Sarah used it as a reminder of what corporate and governmental power could destroy when unopposed.

The lock clicked open.

Inside, organized with scientific precision, lay folders color-coded by content type. Red for internal communications. Blue for engineering reports. Yellow for safety inspections. Green for environmental impact data.

And a single black flash drive taped to the inside lid.

Ruth reached out, her fingers lingering on the drive. "This isn't just evidence. This is memory. The kind they try to drown."

"Start with this," she suggested, carefully removing the drive. "Digital evidence can be copied and secured immediately. Paper can wait."

The clinic's ancient computer hummed to life, its outdated security an unintended advantage against sophisticated corporate hacking. The flash drive contained a single folder labeled with today's date—as if Sarah had predicted exactly when we would be viewing it.

Inside were three files:

LISTEN.mp3 READ.pdf REMEMBER.jpg

I clicked on LISTEN.mp3, bracing myself for Sarah's voice. We met in graduate school—environmental science versus law—and joined forces on a class project about industrial waste disposal in Appalachia. She went corporate, believing she could change the system from within. I went nonprofit, believing the system needed pressure from outside. We argued about our methods but shared a common purpose. Now she was gone, and I sat listening to her final testimony.

"This is Sarah Chen, Environmental Safety Officer for Watershed Management Corporation, employee ID 45723. I'm recording this on March 15th as evidence of criminal negligence and premeditated environmental destruction by Watershed CEO Lawrence Crowder and the executive board."

Another cough, wet and tearing. The sound of tissue against lips. The struggle to breathe. I clenched my fists, anger burning through my chest like the radiation itself.

"For six years, I've documented systematic falsification of safety reports, deliberate weakening of environmental protections, and illegal disposal of toxic materials, including radioactive waste from the company's military contracting division. The retention ponds above Cherokee Valley were designed to fail during the next major precipitation event. This failure is not accidental but engineered to solve two problems for the corporation: costly cleanup of contaminated soil and legal barriers to mineral extraction."

Ruth's fingers paused in their weaving; the pattern momentarily broken as she absorbed the weight of what Sarah had uncovered.

"The attached documents prove that Watershed Management conducted a risk assessment calculating the potential loss of human life against financial benefits. Twenty-six casualties were deemed an 'acceptable loss threshold' compared to the eight billion in mineral rights that would be accessible once the valley was declared uninhabitable and subject to federal disaster acquisition."

Another racking cough interrupted. When Sarah continued, her voice had thinned to a whisper.

"They know I've been collecting evidence. My 'accidental' exposure to radioactive material three weeks ago was no accident. I won't survive to testify. But the evidence will speak for me if it reaches the right hands. Esther—I know you're listening—take this to your grandmother and Dr. Blackfox. They'll know who to trust."

The recording ended with the sound of labored breathing.

I stared at the screen, Sarah's voice still echoing in my ears. For a moment, I couldn't move, rage and grief circling each other like wolves around dying prey. This wasn't just corporate negligence. This was murder. Sarah's murder. Twenty-six predicted deaths. And now thirty-seven actual people—men, women, and children whose names wouldn't appear in Watershed Management's quarterly reports.

"Open the PDF," Mordi said finally, pulling me back to the moment.

I clicked on READ.pdf, revealing a twenty-page document with the Watershed Management logo prominently displayed at the top. Its title, printed in clinical corporate font, read: "Cost-Benefit Analysis: Cherokee Valley Retention System Failure Scenario."

The document methodically outlined the financial advantages of an "engineered environmental event" that would render Cherokee Valley uninhabitable. Cold calculations balanced the cost of wrongful death settlements against the value of mineral deposits that couldn't be accessed through normal channels due to environmental protections and indigenous land claims.

On page seventeen, a highlighted section caught my eye:

"Projected casualty range (15-35 individuals) remains within acceptable loss parameters when balanced against projected revenue from Phase II extraction ($8.2B over 20 years). Recommended course of action is controlled retention failure during the next significant precipitation event. Indigenous land claims become moot under Federal Disaster Acquisition protocols once the valley is classified as a contaminated zone. Legal exposure can be minimized through 'Act of God' classification maintained by our relationships with regulatory agencies."

The final page bore Lawrence Crowder's elegant signature above his typed name and title.

Ruth wove river cane with renewed purpose, her fingers creating a spiral pattern in the basket's center. "The spirals go back to the beginning," she murmured. "They've always calculated our worth against whatever lies beneath our feet. Gold in Georgia. Oil in Oklahoma. Uranium in the Southwest. Rare earths here."

"He signed it," I whispered. "He actually signed the order to kill people for profit."

"They always sign," Ruth said, reaching for another strip of cane. "They believe ink gives them power. They believe paper makes their crimes legal."

Mordi examined the document more closely. "This is on official company documentation with the CEO's signature. This is the smoking gun Sarah died to obtain."

I opened the final file—REMEMBER.jpg.

It was a photograph of Cherokee Valley taken from Rattlesnake Mountain's summit, showing the pristine forest and winding river that had sustained my people for centuries. Superimposed on the image was a map of mining claims and extraction points, transforming the living landscape into measured sections of exploitable resources.

In the corner, handwritten in what I recognized as Sarah's precise script, were the words: "This is what they see when they look at your home. This is why they don't care who dies when the water rises."

"Sarah knew," I said, touching the screen where my friend's handwriting offered one final warning. "She found their plan and knew she'd be silenced."

Ruth finished the spiral pattern in her basket, starting a new one beside it—two spirals connected by a flowing line. "The pattern doesn't just repeat. It evolves. The Georgia militia became federal troops became mining companies became energy corporations became tech giants. Different uniforms. Same hunger."

Outside, thunder rolled across mountains that had witnessed centuries of exploitation. Rain continued falling on a valley deliberately poisoned for profit.

"What happens now?" Mordi asked, pocketing the flash drive copy I'd made for him.

Ruth tied off a section of her basket, marking the completion of one pattern before beginning another. "Now we carry what cannot be drowned. Now we remember what they want forgotten."

The clinic door opened. Jamie stood on the threshold, his expression unreadable. "Esther, we need to talk."

"Come see this first," I said, gesturing toward the computer screen still displaying the incriminating evidence.

"I've already seen it."

The room temperature seemed to drop ten degrees. I moved instinctively toward the strongbox, placing my body between it and Jamie.

"Sarah sent me copies before she died," he continued, stepping into the room and closing the door behind him. "That's why I knew where to find you today. Why I knew the maintenance tunnel code."

"You worked for Watershed," I said, the realization of potential betrayal churning in my stomach. I thought of Lily again—her trust in me to make things right, to protect what couldn't protect itself. I'd failed Sarah. I wouldn't fail my daughter.

"I still do." Jamie's eyes held mine steadily. "But not for Crowder."

He pulled out his wallet and removed an ID card concealed behind his Watershed Management badge. Federal Bureau of Investigation.

"I was assigned to infiltrate Watershed Management three years ago after the EPA flagged irregularities in their waste disposal reporting. Sarah figured out who I was about six months ago. She started passing me evidence, but she didn't trust the normal channels—too many regulators in Watershed's pocket."

"Why tell us now?" Mordi asked, suspicion evident in his voice.

"Because in approximately forty-five minutes, Watershed security will execute a search warrant on this clinic, claiming they're looking for stolen corporate property." Jamie nodded toward the strongbox. "That warrant was signed by Judge Wilson Harrison."

"Crowder's brother-in-law," Ruth said grimly, her fingers never pausing in their weaving.

"We need to move this evidence off-reservation immediately. My handler is waiting at the federal building in Asheville. Once it's in FBI custody with proper chain of evidence documentation, Crowder can't make it disappear."

Ruth's fingers wove faster, creating a pattern that mirrored the valley's waterways. "The same federal government that recognized our sovereignty in one breath and allowed companies to violate it with the next? The same agencies that let mining companies dump waste on our land for decades?"

"Then make copies first," Jamie insisted. "But we need to move."

As Mordi and Jamie began rapidly duplicating documents, I snapped the original flash drive to the chain holding my Cherokee syllabary pendant. Something in Jamie's explanation rang true but incomplete. The FBI might be after Watershed Management, but that didn't mean they would prioritize justice for Cherokee Valley over federal interests.

I thought of Lily again, of the stories I always told her before sleep —about Tsini carrying fire through burning buildings, about water remembering paths that existed before dams, about resistance that outlasts extraction. I owed my daughter more than just survival. I owed her a world where patterns can break, where corporations can't calculate "acceptable losses," where Cherokee land isn't poisoned for profit.

Ruth must have sensed my hesitation. She leaned close, whispering in Cherokee: "Trust the river to remember its path, not the stone to stay unmoved."

I nodded. My grandmother's wisdom crystallized into certainty. Evidence, like water, needed to flow through many channels to reach its destination. Trusting any single authority—even one wearing a badge—meant risking the truth being dammed or diverted.

Ruth's basket now held three connected spiral patterns—past, present, and future woven into a single design. The memory that could not be drowned. The evidence that could not be buried. The pattern emerging despite every attempt to obscure it.

Outside, thunder rumbled across mountains that had witnessed centuries of broken promises. Rain continued falling on a valley deliberately poisoned for profit. And somewhere in Watershed Management's corporate headquarters, Lawrence Crowder was discovering that the evidence he thought safely drowned had surfaced—carried by currents he couldn't control.

The pattern was emerging. But this time, I intended to change the ending.

I placed the strongbox in a waterproof bag, then slid it into my backpack. The weight of thirty-seven deaths—eleven more than Crowder had calculated as "acceptable"—pressed against my spine. I zipped my jacket over the flash drive hanging from my neck, Sarah's voice still echoing in my ears.

"Get that flash drive on the internet," Ruth said, fingers weaving invisible baskets. "Truth, like water, always finds its level."

With one hand, I reached for the clinic door. With the other, I grasped my grandmother's weathered fingers, connecting past resistance to present action.

"Let's go," I said. "The water's rising."

Chapter Three

WHAT SARAH SAW

Three weeks before her death, Sarah's hands still looked human. Not yet translucent, not yet trembling. That came later, after she saw the memo.

I remember her hands vividly—scientist's hands, precise and certain, tapping soil samples into labeled vials like she was playing piano scales. Back before she started coughing blood. Before Watershed Management murdered her with calculated exposure.

Memories flood back as we bolt from the clinic into Ruth's ancient Chevy truck. Its rust-spotted frame vibrates with mountain knowledge the same way my blood now carries radiation. The strongbox sits between us on the cracked vinyl seat, a weight I can't ignore. Rain pounds the roof like judgment.

"Call Caleb at the Smoke Signal," Ruth says, cranking the engine that protests then catches. "Get that flash drive's contents onto their server. They can't shut down tribal media without a federal court order."

I punch numbers into my phone, but reception cuts in and out as we wind up switchbacks away from the valley floor. Water runs in sheets across the road, carrying poison toward communities that don't yet know they've been sacrificed for mineral rights. The call fails three times before it connects.

While Ruth navigates, I remember the last time I saw Sarah alive.

"You shouldn't be here," Sarah whispered, opening her apartment door just wide enough for me to slip through. Three weeks after her "accident" in the lab, her once-vibrant face had hollowed, cheekbones sharp as arrowheads beneath skin gone sallow. The oxygen tank beside her hissed a counter-rhythm to her labored breathing. "They might be watching."

"I brought dinner," I said, holding up the Tupperware of home-made soup like an offering, trying to hide my shock at her deterioration. Sarah had always been strong—five feet two inches of fierce determination. A woman who could hike twelve miles of Appalachian Trail while explaining soil contamination vectors to anyone who'd listen. Now, she moved like someone carrying lead weights.

"Not hungry," she said, though her eyes thanked me. "But I need your help with something more important."

Her apartment struck me as battlefield-sparse—most possessions already sold to cover medical expenses her company insurance suddenly wouldn't cover. On her kitchen table, folders spread in color-coded precision: blue, yellow, red, green. A portable printer hummed in the corner. A stainless steel strongbox waited, lid open.

"The blue folder contains engineering assessments," she explained, voice barely audible above the oxygen concentrator's mechanical rhythm. "Original specifications called for retention walls withstanding 500-year flood events. Watershed secretly modified designs to fail at 50-year events."

She slid the folder into the strongbox with hands that shook slightly, already showing the nerve damage that would worsen in coming days.

"How'd you get these?" I asked, mouth dry with the danger of what I was witnessing.

Sarah's attempt at laughter dissolved into wet coughing that brought pink froth to her lips. I grabbed tissues, gently wiping blood from my friend's mouth while she struggled to breathe. Her skin felt like ancient paper beneath my touch, pulse fluttering erratically against my fingers.

"Turns out dying lowers your risk assessment," she managed once the spasm subsided. "What more can they do to me?"

The yellow folder followed into the box. "Inspection reports—real ones I conducted, showing contamination, and falsified ones they submitted to regulators."

I slid my hand over hers, feeling bones where muscle once was. "Sarah, we need to get you to a hospital."

"For what? So company doctors can write 'idiopathic pulmonary fibrosis' on my chart instead of 'deliberate radiation exposure'?" Her eyes, sunken but clearer than they had any right to be, met mine. "The red folder contains internal communications—emails, meeting minutes, the risk assessment with Crowder's signature authorizing everything."

"This is enough for criminal charges," I said.

"Only if it reaches the right people." Sarah's gaze darted to her apartment window, where rain streaked the glass in patterns that reminded me of tears. "Watershed has influence throughout the regulatory system. The governor's brother sits on their board. Two federal judges have financial interests in the company, including Crowder's brother-in-law."

"We'll take it to the media."

"The parent corporation owns seventeen news outlets in this region." Her laugh turned to coughing again, deeper this time, bringing up more blood.

"I'll file a lawsuit," I persisted, the attorney in me grasping for legal channels even as my heart recognized their inadequacy. "Clean Water Act, RCRA violations—"

"By the time that works through the courts, the valley will be underwater, and thirty-seven people will be dead," Sarah interrupted, precision still evident despite her weakening voice. "Twenty-six in the initial breach, the rest from secondary contamination."

I stared at her. "They calculated that?"

"Like they were ordering office supplies." She pushed a document toward me, where neatly typed casualties appeared in a cost-benefit column. "Projected wrongful death settlements: $26 million. Projected mineral extraction rights: $8.2 billion. Return on investment: approximately 31,500%."

My stomach twisted with nausea that had nothing to do with the medical smells permeating the apartment. "These are people, not numbers."

"Not to Crowder," she said, each word a stone placed deliberately in a wall of evidence. "When I confronted him with the falsified safety reports, he called it 'standard industry practice.' When I mentioned the risk to the reservation, he said indigenous land claims were 'temporary inconveniences' in the resource development timeline."

She closed the strongbox but didn't lock it. "I'm not finished yet. There's one more document I need—proof that the military contracting division has been illegally disposing of radioactive waste in the north retention pond. It connects Watershed's environmental crimes to national security interests." Sarah's breathing labored further. "Getting it will be dangerous."

"Let me do it," I offered immediately.

"No. I'm already dying. They made sure of that when I started asking questions." Her gaze drifted to the window, where rain had begun falling on mountains soon to be transformed by corporate greed. "If I don't come back from the facility tomorrow night, the combination is the date of the Treaty of New Echota."

"The removal treaty," I whispered, recognizing the historical significance—a document that had led to the Trail of Tears, another calculated sacrifice of Cherokee lives for others' profit.

"History repeats itself," Sarah said. "Different weapons, same war." She reached for my hand, her grip surprisingly strong. "Promise me you'll finish this. Promise me they won't just wash away what happened here under 'Acts of God' and 'regrettable tragedies.'"

"I promise," I said, the oath settling into my bones. "Whatever it takes."

Sarah nodded, temporarily satisfied. Then she leaned forward, urgency overtaking exhaustion. "There's something else you need to know. Something I discovered in their geological surveys."

"What?"

"The minerals they want to extract? They're directly beneath the sacred mound."

Ruth swerves the truck onto a logging road as headlights appear behind us, cutting through the rain with predatory focus. My memory shatters, present danger crowding out past conversations.

"Watershed security," she mutters, hands steady on the wheel as we bounce over ruts that would cripple the pursuit vehicle's lower clearance. "They move fast for corporate types."

I glance back at the strongbox wedged against my thigh, thinking of Sarah's final warning about the mound. The pieces connect in my radiation-altered blood with certainty beyond evidence. What they're after isn't just access to minerals—it's something beneath our most sacred site, something they believe worth thirty-seven calculated deaths.

My phone chimes—the transfer to the tribal newspaper is complete. Truth finding new channels, beginning to flow beyond strongboxes and flash drives into streams that corporate dams can't contain.

"We need to get to the mound," I tell Ruth, decision crystallizing even as I speak. "Not just because of the evidence. Because of what's beneath it."

Ruth's eyes never leave the treacherous road, but her mouth curves slightly. "I was wondering when you'd figure that out."

"Sarah knew. That's why they killed her—not just for documenting the planned flood, but for discovering what they really want."

The truck crests a ridge, and suddenly the valley spreads below us. Even through darkness and sheeting rain, I can see floodwaters gleaming like black silk in the moonlight, contamination spreading exactly as Sarah predicted. Near the valley's heart, industrial lights blaze against the sacred mound—metal against memory, temporary against eternal.

My blood hums with knowledge passed from Tsini through generations. This isn't just about evidence anymore. This is about what lies beneath that mound—something the mountain has protected for centuries, something corporate men with extraction equipment are now attempting to violate.

"We won't let them," I say, hand moving to the flash drive still hanging around my neck. "Sarah didn't die for nothing."

Ruth nods, turning the truck toward the mound where bulldozers already scar sacred earth. "The pattern tries to repeat," she says, fingers tapping the steering wheel in a rhythm my blood recognizes. "But this time, we change the ending."

The strongbox shifts against my leg as we descend toward confrontation, its weight a promise I made to Sarah, to my daughter, to ancestors who carried fire through flames and truth through genocide. The radiation in my blood sings strange harmonies with mountain memory, with a determination that runs deeper than fear or pain or death itself.

I finger the scar on my palm—legacy of a girlhood fall on these same slopes, a blood offering that connected me to this land long before I understood what that meant. Now my blood carries poison that should kill me but instead seems to be transforming something essential in my cells. I'm becoming a different kind of vessel—not just for evidence but for mountain memory itself.

The headlights behind us have disappeared, but I harbor no illusion they've given up. Corporate security knows exactly where we're heading. They'll be waiting at the mound, prepared to protect billions in mineral rights with whatever force necessary.

But they've miscalculated something essential. They've run their risk assessments assuming opponents who fear death more than injustice. They've calculated resistance based on individuals, not on patterns that flow through generations.

I touch the strongbox, feeling Sarah's presence in the evidence she died collecting. "I'm coming," I whisper, though whether to Sarah or the mound or whatever lies beneath it, I'm not entirely sure.

The truck lurches forward, and I brace against the dashboard. Ahead, excavation equipment looms against sacred stone. Behind us, security forces regroup. The rain continues falling, cleansing what it can, carrying memory through channels older than any human map.

The pattern repeats, but this time I stand where Sarah fell. This time, I carry evidence in a strongbox and determination in every cell.

This time, the mountain might just find the voice it needs.

Chapter Four

NETWORKS OF RESISTANCE

The federal building smelled like paper and power—the peculiar scent of systems designed to process truth into manageable documents.

Rain streaked the bulletproof glass as we hurried through security. Ruth's silver hair dripped onto marble floors polished to reflect institutional authority back at itself. The strongbox pressed against my spine through the waterproof bag, thirty-seven deaths weighing more with each step. The flash drive burned against my chest, Sarah's voice still echoing in my ears.

Jamie led us across the vast atrium where American flags hung motionless in climate-controlled air, their colors too bright against gray stone walls. His back rigid, shoulders squared to FBI standards. The security badges around our necks marked us as variables allowed temporary admission to the equation.

"Ninth floor," Jamie said, swiping his credentials at a private elevator. "Agent Morrison has a secure evidence room ready."

"How many people know we're coming?" I asked, the radiation in my blood making me hypersensitive to threat, to betrayal, to patterns repeating through institutional hallways.

"Just Morrison and his direct supervisor." The doors slid closed. "Chain of custody has to be impeccable for evidence this explosive.

One procedural mistake and Watershed's lawyers will bury it in motions for years."

The elevator hummed upward, the floors ticking past like a countdown. Ruth caught my eye, her left hand working invisible river cane, weaving patterns that spoke what her lips wouldn't with Jamie present. Multiple channels. Don't trust a single path.

My phone vibrated. An email notification from Caleb at the Smoke Signal: Transfer complete. Files backed up on four servers. Working on verification before publishing.

One channel flowing. But not enough.

The elevator stopped at four instead of nine.

"This isn't our floor," Jamie said, frowning as the doors opened.

The woman waiting wore a charcoal pantsuit and a formal demeanor, but something in her stance triggered warning bells. Her eyes tracked straight to the backpack containing Sarah's strongbox, barely registering our faces.

"Agent Redhawk," she said. "Agent Morrison sent me to escort you to the alternate secure room. There's been a location change."

Jamie's hesitation lasted one heartbeat too long. "ID?" he asked, his hand drifting toward his weapon.

The woman's smile never reached her eyes. "Laurel Kline, Assistant Director. We met at the Louisville conference." She flashed her credentials too quickly for verification. "Security concerns. The Director authorized the change five minutes ago."

I felt Ruth stiffen beside me. My grandmother had testified before too many congressional committees not to recognize bureaucratic choreography disguising threat.

"I'll call Morrison to confirm," Jamie said, reaching for his phone.

"Communications blackout during evidence transfer," Kline countered smoothly. "Standard protocol for cases involving national security."

She stepped onto the elevator. The doors closed. We were in motion again but now descending rather than climbing.

"Watershed knows we're here," I whispered, certainty flowing through my radiation-altered blood. "This isn't FBI."

Kline's hand moved toward her jacket. The elevator stopped

between floors with a jolt that sent us staggering. Emergency lights clicked on, bathing everything in blood-red.

"The strongbox," Kline demanded, dropping the federal mask as she pulled a pistol. "Now."

Jamie shoved himself between Kline and us, his FBI training engaging even as confusion played across his features. "What the hell? You're not Assistant Director—"

"Watershed Corporate Security," she cut him off. "And you're not just FBI, are you, Jamie? My team tracked your encrypted transmissions to Sarah Chen for months. Playing both sides is dangerous work."

The revelation crystallized in the elevator's red emergency lighting. Jamie—not fully FBI, not fully Watershed—had been caught by an entity that would sacrifice him without hesitation.

"Give me the evidence," Kline continued, her gun steady on Jamie's chest. "Nobody needs to die in this elevator."

The irony struck me like a physical blow. Nobody needs to die. Thirty-seven people already had.

"The strongbox contains proof of premeditated murder," I said, anger burning through caution. "Crowder signed the order to kill twenty-six people for mineral rights."

"Thirty-seven," Kline corrected with the same casual indifference Crowder had shown. "The revised count came in this morning. Still within acceptable parameters."

Ruth made a small sound beside me—not fear but recognition of patterns repeating. The Treaty of New Echota all over again. Different weapons. Same calculation of indigenous lives against resource extraction.

"The evidence is already out," I said. "Multiple copies have beendistributed through secured channels."

"Digital copies can be discredited. Witnesses intimidated." Kline's eyes never left the backpack. "Original documents with corporate letterhead and authenticated signatures—those are harder to dismiss. The strongbox, please."

My fingers brushed the cool metal of Sarah's flash drive hanging around my neck. I thought of Lily, of the future waiting in her copper hair and small hands that already knew how to listen when mountains speak.

The elevator's emergency panel offered only an illusion of help. Even if we could call out, who would answer? What system would intervene against corporate interest?

"When federal agents find three bodies in this elevator," Kline continued, "the official report will cite unfortunate mechanical failure. Tragic but unavoidable."

Jamie shifted his weight subtly. FBI training preparing for confrontation in confined space. "You won't get away with this,"he said, words so similar to those in a television show that they seemed almost comical in this red-lit coffin.

"Watershed Security has managed more complex situations." Kline's smile returned, professional and empty. "The evidence, please. I won't ask again."

The radiation in my blood hummed strange frequencies, alerting me to dangers beyond the obvious. Whatever happened in this elevator, the truth needed to survive. Memory needed to continue. The pattern needed to break, not just repeat with different casualties.

Ruth's hand found mine, her weathered fingers pressing a small object into my palm—the fire striker she always carried, a legacy of ancestors who preserved flame through forced marches and government schools.

"Trust the river," she whispered in Cherokee. "Not the stone."

I dropped to the floor as she pressed the emergency alarm. The shrieking filled our metal cage as Jamie launched himself at Kline. The gun discharged with a deafening crack in the confined space— but Jamie had disrupted her aim. The bullet punched into the ceiling.

The backpack slipped from my shoulders. I pulled Sarah's flash drive from around my neck and pressed it into Ruth's hand while Kline and Jamie grappled for the weapon.

"Get this out," I yelled over the alarm. "I'll protect the strongbox."

Ruth nodded, understanding flowing between us. The evidence needed multiple channels. No single path could be trusted.

Another shot. Jamie cried out, clutching his shoulder where blood bloomed across his shirt. Kline turned toward me, her composure fractured into something feral and focused.

Just then, red turned to darkness as the elevator's power cut completely.

In the sudden black, I struck Ruth's fire starter against the metal flooring. Sparks illuminated shocked faces for microseconds. Darkness again. Another strike. More sparks. The alarm continued its electronic scream.

"Drop your weapon," a new voice commanded as the elevator doors were forced open from outside. Flashlight beams cut through the darkness, revealing Morrison and two agents on the floor below, weapons drawn.

Kline's gun clattered to the floor.

"Agent Morrison," she said, switching masks yet again. "Thank god you're here. These people stole classified corporate documents—"

"Save it," Morrison cut her off. "Your credentials are fake, and we have your conversation recorded. Hands behind your back."

Light returned—regular fluorescents replacing emergency red. Ruth stood calmly in the corner, flash drive nowhere to be seen. Jamie pressed a hand to his bleeding shoulder. Kline's confidentdemeanor collapsed completely as agents secured her wrists with plastic restraints.

"Watershed employs seventy-three federal judges and two hundred congressional staffers," she hissed. "You think this evidence will ever see trial?"

"I think truth, like water, finds its level," Ruth said, the basket-weaver's philosophy silencing corporate threat more effectively than any legal counter.

Morrison helped Jamie to a sitting position, barking orders for medical assistance. "We need to move quickly," he told me. "Kline wasn't working alone. There will be others."

"The flash drive—" I began.

"Is already being uploaded to secure Justice Department servers," Ruth said. Her eyes held mine with centuries of Cherokee resistance. The drive hadn't disappeared; it had gone where Watershed couldn't follow.

"The original documents need protection until authenticated," Morrison explained, nodding toward the strongbox now visible in my open backpack. "We have a secure room prepared with continuous video monitoring and multiple witnesses from different agencies."

Ruth's fingers continued their invisible weaving, creating patterns that mapped right action. "Can we trust him?" I asked her in Cherokee.

"No single channel," she responded in the same. "But this one flows toward justice for now."

I felt the weight of choices across generations—from Tsini rescuing fire to Sarah documenting corporate crime to my own decision in this elevator. Different moments, same pattern: carrying truth through systems designed to drown it.

"Let's go," I said, retrieving the backpack as medical personnel swarmed around Jamie. "But I'm not leaving the evidence until it's properly documented by multiple parties."

Radiation pulsed through my bloodstream, accelerating damage while heightening awareness. Cold sweat beaded my forehead. Metallic taste coated my tongue. My vision blurred then sharpened to unnatural clarity. The symptoms were worsening even as they transformed me into something else—not just a victim but a vessel for mountain memory.

As we followed Morrison to the secure evidence room, Ruth leaned close. "Sarah knew this would happen," she whispered. "That's why she created multiple paths for truth. Like water finding channels through stone."

"Even if they block every official channel—" I started.

"Truth rises," Ruth finished simply. "It always does."

In the evidence room, I placed the strongbox on a steel table beneath unblinking camera eyes. I unsealed it for Morisson, allowing him to remove each color-coded folder with gloved hands while a stenographer recorded detailed descriptions. Each document linking Watershed Management to the deaths of thirty-seven people—soon to be more as toxins spread through groundwater and soil.

My nose began to bleed, red droplets spattering official forms. Not from motion or stress—from radiation transforming my cells into something institutional medicine couldn't categorize.

Mordi's warnings echoed in my head. The exposure levels when I retrieved the strongbox. The accelerated cellular damage. The shortened lifespan now measuring my days.

But standing there, watching truth enter the official record, I felt strangely peaceful. I had carried forward what Sarah couldn't. Had created channels corporate dams couldn't block. Had ensured the pattern wouldn't simply repeat unchallenged.

"We need to get you to a hospital," Morrison said, noticing the blood.

"Not yet," I replied, wiping crimson from my lips. "First, I need to know this evidence is secure."

The door burst open. Two men in dark suits with FBI credentials entered, their stance revealing military training beneath federal badges.

"Agent Morrison," the taller one announced, "this evidence is being reclassified under national security protocols. The materials found at Watershed Management's facility contained elements of interest to the Defense Department."

Morrison stepped forward, institutional confusion written across his face. "I received no such orders. This is an active homicide investigation—"

"Orders come directly from the Director," the agent cut him off. "These materials are now classified beyond your security clearance."

Ruth's eyes met mine. The pattern repeating. Exploitative power shifting masks—from corporate security to government authority—but always protecting extraction over life.

"Thirty-seven people died," I said, blood from my nose staining my collar. "This isn't about national security. It's about corporate murder."

"Ma'am, please step away from the evidence," the second agent said, hand resting on his weapon. "This is now a matter of federal security."

Morrison looked trapped between duty and conscience, institutional loyalty battling witnessed truth. "Let me see the orders," he demanded.

While they argued jurisdiction, Ruth moved closer to the evidence table where the strongbox sat open, its contents now spread for documentation. Her hands never stopped their basket-weaving motions, sweeping the contents in the box. Theseinvisible patterns mapped flow through resistance. The box was no longer on the table, now in her capable hands.

I wasn't raised to fear death. I was raised to fear leaving work unfinished.

The memory of these words—my own from just hours ago—steadied me. The radiation in my blood wasn't just killing me. It was connecting me to something larger than my individual body, just as the living flame Tsini rescued wasn't extinguished with her death.

I leaned toward Ruth. "The mound," I whispered. "We need to get to the sacred mound."

She nodded once, understanding immediately. "That's what they really want. What Sarah discovered in their geological surveys."

The argument between Morrison and the new agents escalated, jurisdiction disputes masking the actual conflict—truth versus power, memory versus extraction, pattern recognized versus pattern repeated.

"We need to move now," Ruth murmured. "While they're distracted."

We backed toward the door, silent as night hunters. The surveillance cameras would record our departure, but by the time anyone noticed, we'd be gone—carrying truth through different channels than official documentation could track.

In the hallway, Ruth pulled me toward service stairs rather than elevators. Decades of tribal activism had taught her every government building had back ways out, paths not monitored with the same attention as main entrances.

"Where is your truck?" I asked as we descended, each step sending sharp pain through my radiation-altered nervous system.

"East parking garage. Second level." Ruth moved with surprising speed for eighty-two years, her body remembering patterns of escape from protests decades past.

My phone vibrated. A text from an unknown number: Morrison stalling them. Evidence being copied by trusted assistant. Get to mound. Will meet you there.

"Jamie?" I asked Ruth, showing her the message.

"Or trap," she responded, ever practical. "Trust the water, not the single stone."

We reached the parking level, slipping between vehicles toward Ruth's ancient Chevy. My vision swam with each step, radiation damage accelerating through exertion. Blood dripped steadily from my nose now, marking our path like crimson breadcrumbs.

Once inside the truck, Ruth started the engine, which protested and then caught with its familiar determination. "The mound,"she confirmed, pulling out of the space with a deliberate calm that would attract less attention than a rushed escape.

"That's where they're extracting," I said, understanding crystallizing through pain. "Not just rare earth minerals. Something else. Something beneath the sacred site that connects to what's changing in my blood."

Ruth nodded, navigating through downtown traffic with studied normality. "Sarah called me the night before she died. Said Watershed found something in core samples that military contractors want. Something that responds to specific genetic markers."

"Cherokee markers," I whispered, remembering Sarah's final warning.

"That's why they calculate our lives as acceptable losses," Ruth said, turning onto the highway that would take us back toward the reservation. "They believe whatever lies beneath the mound is worth more than the people who've protected it for centuries."

In the side mirror, I spotted a black SUV matching our turns, maintaining precise distance. Federal technique for surveillance without alerting the target.

"We're being followed," I said.

"I know." Ruth's eyes never left the road. "They always follow. That's part of the pattern too."

The radiation in my blood sang strange harmonies with the mountain's approaching proximity. My cells weren't just dying; they were transforming into something institutional science couldn't classify. The damage was accelerating even as it created new pathways for perception.

"We won't reach the mound before they catch us," I said, practical assessment rather than fear.

"We don't need to." Ruth turned suddenly onto a logging road barely visible between crowding pines. "Water finds channels stones can't block."

The truck bounced over ruts as we climbed away from the main highway. Behind us, the SUV slowed, too wide for the narrow track, its federal driver recalculating approach.

"This leads to Thunder Ridge," Ruth explained, hands steady on the wheel despite the treacherous path. "There's a trail down the back side that connects to the mound. A path not on government maps."

Blood dripped steadily from my nose, spattering my shirt, the seat, the floor mats. Each bump sent daggers through my nervous system. But my mind remained clear—clearer than before, as if radiation were burning away everything except essential understanding.

"If I don't make it—" I began.

"You'll finish what Sarah started," Ruth interrupted. "Different form, maybe. But you'll finish it."

The certainty in her voice steadied me. Ruth had witnessed cycles of exploitation and resistance across eight decades. Had seen how patterns repeat but also how they evolve. Had carried ancestral knowledge through systems designed to erase it.

"Crowder will be at the mound," I said, realization flowing through altered blood. "Personally overseeing extraction of whatever they found beneath it."

"Good." Ruth's smile contained no mirth, only recognition. "Then he'll witness what happens when the mountain answers."

The truck crested the ridge. Below us spread Cherokee Valley, partly submerged beneath toxic floodwater, exactly as Sarah had predicted. Near its heart, the sacred mound rose like an island of memory in a sea of forgetting. Industrial lights blazed against its slopes, excavation equipment scarring soil that had witnessed a thousand years of ceremony.

"They're moving faster than I expected," Ruth said, scanning the activity below. "They know we have the evidence. They're trying to extract what they can before legal channels can stop them."

I wiped blood from my face with a sleeve already soaked crimson. "How do we get down there?"

Ruth pointed to a barely visible trail snaking down the ridge's far side. "That path follows water's memory. It will take us behind their security perimeter."

The black SUV appeared on the main road below, federal agents scanning the ridge with binoculars. They hadn't spotted us yet, but they would soon.

"We need to move," Ruth said, killing the engine. "Can you walk?"

The question wasn't condescension but a practical assessment. My radiation sickness had accelerated beyond what Mordi had predicted, blood now seeping from my gums, vision blurring then sharpening to painful clarity.

"I'll walk," I said, opening the door. "And if I can't walk, I'll crawl."

The mountain air hit my lungs like electricity, each breath amplifying the connection between my altered cells and the ancient stone beneath my feet. The radiation wasn't just poison; it was a translator, opening pathways between human consciousness and geological memory.

We moved onto the trail, Ruth leading with confidence born from decades of walking these slopes. My steps faltered but found a rhythm in necessity. Each footfall connected me to generations who had traveled this same path—from Tsini carrying fire to Ruth carrying legal briefs to my own journey to this moment.

"The path remembers even when maps forget," Ruth said, her voice blending with the wind through pine needles and distant thunder. "That's how our people survived. Memory carried through channels the government couldn't monitor."

The trail descended sharply, following a stream bed that had been dry for generations but was still etched into the mountain's skin. My feet knew where to step without conscious direction, as if ancestral knowledge flowed upward through the soil into myblood.

Halfway down, Ruth pulled me behind a granite outcropping. Below, security personnel patrolled with tactical precision, their movements illuminated by industrial lights surrounding the mound.

"Watershed's private military," Ruth observed. "Ex-special forces mostly. They guard extraction sites worldwide."

My vision swam, then stabilized with unnatural clarity. I could see details I shouldn't—the ceramic plates in their tactical vests, the radio frequencies blinking on their communication devices, the pattern of their patrol routes.

"There," I whispered, pointing to a drainage culvert built into the mound's western base. "That's our way in. The water channel. They're not watching it."

Ruth studied my face, recognition dawning in her eyes. "You see it differently now, don't you? The radiation's changing your perception."

I nodded, unable to explain how cellular damage had become a pathway to a new perspective. "I can see the patterns they can't. The channels water remembers."

We continued downward, using trees for cover, moving only when patrols turned away. The excavation site grew more visible with each step—equipment assembled with military efficiency, core samples labeled and secured in specialized containers, and technicians working under portable laboratory tents.

At the base of the ridge, we paused behind a fallen oak, its massive trunk providing final cover before the exposed approach to the drainage culvert. Two hundred feet of open ground separated us from our target. Two hundred feet where corporate security would spot us immediately.

"We need a distraction," Ruth said, calculating with the strategic patience of someone who had faced down federal agents at pipeline protests and uranium mine blockades.

Thunder rumbled closer, rain beginning again as if responding to an unspoken request. The mountain coordinating the defense of its own memory.

"Give me your necklace," Ruth said suddenly, eyes on my silver chain that held my Cherokee syllabary pendant.

I slipped it over my head, watching as she attached the fire striker to it. "What are you—"

"Creating another channel," she said, wrapping the chain around a rock, then calculating a trajectory. "Truth flows between systems that try to control or contain it."

With surprising strength, Ruth hurled the rock and striker far to our right—where it clattered against equipment

With surprising strength, Ruth hurled the rock and striker far to our right—where it clattered against equipment near the generator powering industrial lights.

The effect was immediate. Security personnel turned toward the sound, weapons drawn, flashlights scanning for the source. Three moved to investigate, approaching with tactical caution. The channel to the drainage culvert was temporarily cleared.

"Now," Ruth whispered.

We sprinted across open ground, my radiation-weakened body fueled by a determination that burned hotter than cellular damage. Rain intensified as we ran, as if the mountain coordinated all elements in its defense.

The culvert opening appeared before us—an ancient stone arch incorporated into a modern drainage system. The security teamwas still focused on Ruth's distraction, their backs to our approach. Twenty feet. Ten. Five.

We slipped into the darkness of the tunnel passage, the smell of wet stone and mineral-rich earth replacing industrial diesel and disturbed soil. Water flowed around our ankles, its path worn through centuries of mountain memory.

"This way," I whispered, cellular connection to the mountain mapping passages security engineers had categorized as separate, but the living stone recognized as unified. "The tunnel leads directly beneath the excavation site."

Ruth followed as I navigated twisting passages that narrowed then widened according to water's ancient wisdom rather than human design efficiency. Above us, boots thudded on packed earth, voices murmured with corporate purpose, and machines growled with extraction hunger.

The tunnel ended at a maintenance grate that offered a view of the mound's summit. There, beneath portable floodlights, stood Lawrence Crowder himself—immaculate in a tailored suit despite rain and mud, examining core samples with the detached interest of someone calculating value against quarterly projections.

Beside him, scientists in Watershed lab coats huddled over equipment that hummed with purpose I could feel through the stone beneath my palms. They weren't just measuring; they were activating something. Waking what should remain sleeping.

I pressed against the grate. It gave slightly, metal hasp loose against ancient stone that remembered what belonged and what didn't.

"What do you see?" Ruth asked, her eyes less adapted to the darkness than mine.

Blood dripped steadily from my nose, from my ears now, marking stone that had seen other sacrifices across centuries. "They're drilling directly into the mound's center," I whispered. "But that's not all. They've found something. Something that glows blue-green when Crowder touches it."

My altered blood responded as I spoke, pulsing with the same frequency as the sample in Crowder's manicured hands. Not coincidence. Recognition.

With one push, the grate swung open. Not locked at all, but held by the corporate assumption that separation meant security. That categorization equaled control.

"Stay here," I told Ruth, already slipping through the opening. "If I don't come back—"

"You'll find another channel," she finished with absolute certainty. "Like water. Like memory. Like truth."

I emerged behind equipment staging, shadows gathering me into their protection. The rain fell harder now, driving security personnel toward shelter, scientists huddling over delicate instruments, Crowder alone remaining unmoved at the center of industrial violation.

I moved upward, body pressed against the mound's surface, blood marking sacred soil in a pattern older than the Treaty of New Echota, older than America itself. Each step connected me to Tsini, to Ruth, to generations who had protected this place against forces that calculated extraction above relationship.

At the summit, Crowder stood alone, rain plastering his expensive suit against his corporate frame. He had his back to my approach as he studied blue-green material extracted from the mound's heart. The same blue-green that now pulsed through my radiation-altered blood.

"It's not yours to take," I said, my voice carrying above machine growl and rain percussion.

Crowder turned, surprise briefly crossing features trained to mask reaction. "Ms. Nighthawk," he said, corporate mask reasserting itself. "I was wondering when you'd arrive. Your radiation badge suggests you shouldn't be alive, yet here you are."

"I'm not the first Cherokee to survive what your kind calculated as certain death," I responded, blood running freely down my chin now, marking the ground between us.

His eyes tracked the crimson path, scientific curiosity momentarily overcoming corporate caution. "You're experiencing cellular transformation, aren't you? The same properties we've observed in the core samples. Radiation damage creating new neural pathways rather than destroying existing ones."

"You know what's happening to me," I realized, the truth flowing through altered blood. "You've seen it before. In Sarah."

"Dr. Chen was our first documented case," Crowder acknowledged, rain streaming down his face like tears his kind never shed. "After accidental exposure, her deterioration followed expected patterns until she handled these samples. Then something changed. Her cellular structure began reconfiguring instead of breaking down."

"So you killed her before she could document the connection," I said, rage burning through radiation sickness. "Before she could expose that you've known about the living stone's properties all along."

Crowder's smile contained no warmth, only calculation. "The material beneath this mound represents the largest deposit of non-terrestrial rare earth elements ever discovered. Elements with properties that respond to specific genetic markers." His eyes measured me like core sample. "Cherokee markers."

The revelation landed like a physical blow. Not just minerals. Not just water. Something the mountain had protected for centuries because it responded to bloodlines connected to this specific place.

"You can feel it, can't you?" he continued, scientific fascination battling corporate containment. "The cellular communication. The molecular restructuring. The bridge forming between human consciousness and geological memory. Dr. Chen could. And now you."

"That's why you calculated our deaths as acceptable," I said, understanding crystallizing through pain. "You needed the reservation empty. Needed Cherokee bloodlines removed from proximity to the living stone."

"Indigenous land claims are temporary inconveniences in resource development timelines," Crowder confirmed, repeating what he'd told Sarah weeks before her death. "The flood created necessary legal circumstances for federal disaster acquisition. Once declared a contamination zone, this entire valley falls under emergency management protocols—circumventing tribal sovereignty entirely."

I laughed—a sound like creek water downstream from mine tailings. "You miscalculated."

"Did we?" Crowder gestured to the equipment surrounding the mound, the security forces securing the perimeter, the extraction already in progress. "Your evidence is being classified under national security protocols even now. Your radiation sickness gives you days at most. The tribal evacuation is eighty percent complete." His corporate confidence returned fully. "I'd say our calculations remain within acceptable parameters."

As he spoke, I felt something shifting beneath us—not a physical movement but energy changing state. The blue-green sample in his hand pulsed stronger, synchronizing with the blood now flowing freely from my nose, my ears, and my eyes. Not just radiation damage but communication. Connection between human sacrifice and mountain memory.

"You've analyzed the material composition," I said, stalling while the energy continued building beneath our feet. "But have you considered its consciousness?"

Crowder's expression shifted from corporate certainty to scientific caution. "Consciousness is not a property of geological formations."

"Neither is blue-green luminescence that responds to genetic markers," I countered. "Neither is molecular restructuring that communicates across separate samples. Neither is radiation resistance that transforms cellular damage into perceptual pathways."

The ground trembled slightly. Not earthquake but recognition. The mountain listening through stone older than human language.

Around us, scientists looked up from instruments, suddenly registering impossible data. Security personnel touched their earpieces after receiving concerning reports. Equipment faltered, readings spiked, and communications stuttered.

Crowder's hand tightened around the core sample, corporate control battling forces beyond quarterly projection. "Whatever you think is happening, Ms. Nighthawk, it doesn't change the fundamental economics. This material is worth trillions. Worth thirty-seven deaths. Worth an entire contaminated valley."

"You still believe you're in control," I said, blood rolling down my face like ceremonial paint. "Still believe extraction only flows one direction."

As I spoke, the blue-green material in Crowder's hand flared brighter, energy pulsing with each word. Not random. Responsive. My radiation-altered blood communicating directly with what the mountain had protected for centuries.

Crowder looked from the sample to my bleeding face, corporate certainty giving way to scientific alarm. "What are you doing?"

"I'm not doing anything," I said truthfully. "The mountain is remembering. The pattern is changing."

A security officer approached, radio crackling with static that formed words in no human language. "Sir, we're getting unusual readings from all sample sites. The material is becoming unstable."

Around us, equipment shuddered as if caught in winds that didn't touch human skin. Computer screens flashed with data that shouldn't exist. Communication devices broadcast frequencies that carried no human speech but pulsed with mountain memory.

"Secure the samples," Crowder ordered, his voice steady but eyes revealing the first fractures in corporate certainty. "Full containment protocols."

But blue-green light now emanated from the mound itself—not just core samples but the entire sacred site pulsing with energy that responded to my presence, to my blood freely flowing onto soil that recognized its own.

Scientists backed away from instruments that crossed from controlled experiments to witnessed phenomena beyond institutional classification. Security personnel raised weapons against threats they couldn't target or contain.

And still I stood at the center, blood marking patterns on stone that had witnessed centuries of ceremony, of protection, of relationship corporate extraction could never categorize or control.

"It's over, Crowder," I said, my voice carrying through rain suddenly fallen silent, through machines suddenly stilled, through corporate calculation suddenly irrelevant.

"It's not over until I say it's over," he insisted, but the words sounded hollow even to his ears. His hands shook slightly—not with fear but with recognition that systems he trusted had encountered forces they couldn't process.

The blue-green light intensified, spreading from the core samples into the mound itself, into the soil beneath excavation equipment, into water flowing through channels older than human settlement. Not random illumination but deliberate communication—the mountain speaking through means beyond language.

The ground beneath us shuddered—not collapsing but awakening. Fissures opened in perfect spiral patterns that exactly matched the designs Ruth wove into river cane baskets, that appeared in Cherokee pottery fragments thousands of years old, that flowed through my radiation-altered blood in molecular restructuring beyond scientific classification.

"Full evacuation," Crowder ordered, corporate control transforming into survival instinct. "Secure all samples and data. Implement containment protocols."

Scientists abandoned their equipment, security personnel retreated down the mound's slopes, extraction machinery stood silent as the blue-green light continued spreading—not just through stone but through air, through rain now falling again, through connections invisible to instruments but clear to blood that recognized its source.

As corporate personnel fled, Ruth appeared from the maintenance tunnel, her straight-backed dignity unmoved by thepanic around her.

She walked directly to where I stood bleeding onto sacred soil, her weathered hands steady as she reached for mine.

"The pattern never just repeats," she said, watching blue-green light now flowing like water through channels corporate calculation had attempted to control. "It evolves."

Crowder backed away, the core sample in his hand now pulsing with energy that responded not to his touch but to the mountain's memory rising through stone, through soil, through blood that carried ancestral recognition.

"This changes nothing," he insisted, even as evidence of thelimitations of his worldview surrounded him in living light. "The legal machinery is already in motion. The federal classification order signed. The extraction permits secured."

"You still don't understand," Ruth said, voice carrying the weight of eight decades watching systems rise and fall while the mountain remained. "This was never about your permission or paperwork. This is about water finding its level. About truth rising through channels you can't contain."

The blue-green light reached its crescendo, surrounding us in a radiance that connected blood and stone and water in patterns corporate categorization could never map or monitor.

In that illumination, Crowder saw fully for the first time—not just an extraction opportunity but a living relationship his systems had calculated as irrelevant. Not a resource but a consciousness that had chosen its own protector long before corporate structures existed.

"What is happening here?" he asked, corporate mask fallen completely, revealing only a man confronting a force his quarterly reports couldn't accommodate.

"The mountain is remembering," I answered, blood flowing freely but pain receding as the blue-green energy moved through my altered cells, restructuring what radiation had damaged, creating communication where corporate calculation had predicted only destruction.

Ruth's hand squeezed mine, ancestral knowledge flowing between us—grandmother to granddaughter, past to present, pattern recognized to pattern transformed.

"And so are we," she added simply.

The light began to recede, drawing back into the mound, into the soil, into the water running through channels older than human settlement. But where it passed, it left change—not just in illumination but in the relationship between elements corporate extraction had categorized as separate but the mountain recognized as unified.

As darkness returned, Crowder stood abandoned by security forces, by scientists, by extraction equipment. All now stood silent in the rain. It was just man against mountain, corporate calculation against memory that outlasted systems designed to control or contain it.

"This evidence will never reach court," he said, making a final attempt to assert patterns that had always worked before. "The classification order—"

"Is irrelevant," I finished. "The evidence is already flowing through channels your systems can't control. The truth about thethirty-seven deaths. The intentional flood. The toxic poison. The attempted theft of sacred ground."

Ruth stepped forward, her eighty-two years carried with dignity no corporate power could diminish. "You calculated our lives as acceptable losses," she said, each word a stone placed deliberately in a wall of truth corporate documents couldn't bury. "But water doesn't recognize your barriers. Truth rises, no matter what systems try to contain it."

The sound of approaching vehicles broke the moment—not Watershed security returning but tribal police and federal agents arriving simultaneously, Morrison at their lead with weapon drawn and institutional certainty temporarily aligned with witnessed justice.

"Lawrence Crowder," Morrison announced, "you're under arrest for thirty-seven counts of negligent homicide, environmental terrorism, and conspiracy against tribal sovereignty."

Crowder's shoulders sagged imperceptibly—not surrender but recognition that patterns he controlled had themselves been disrupted by forces his systems couldn't process or contain. "My attorneys will have me released before morning," he said, corporate reflex asserting itself even in defeat.

"Perhaps," Morrison acknowledged, securing restraints around corporate wrists. "But the evidence is already flowing through multiple channels—it is being considered at the federal level and within tribal courts. Your guilt is being carried on a wave of bothofficial reports and through networks your containment can never fully block."

As they led Crowder away, Ruth and I stood on the mound's summit watching industrial dismantling begin—federal agents securing extraction equipment, tribal authorities establishing a perimeter, scientists cataloging damage while trying to classify what they had witnessed.

The blue-green light had receded completely now, but its effects remained—not just in illumination but in relationship between elements corporate extraction had calculated as separate but the mountain recognized as unified.

"Look," Ruth said, pointing toward soil where Watershed had begun drilling. From disturbed earth, tiny blue-green shoots emerged —plants unlike any with a current botanical classification, following spiral patterns identical to Ruth's basket designs. Not random growth but a deliberate response, the mountain's memory finding new expression through channels corporate contamination had inadvertently opened.

My blood still flowed, marking sacred ground with sacrifice freely given rather than calculatedly taken. But the pain had receded, replaced by clarity beyond institutional medicine's ability to measure or monitor.

"The radiation damage in my blood," I said, understanding flowing through altered cells. "It's not killing me. Not exactly."

Ruth nodded, witnessing transformation beyond medical categorization with the calm acceptance of someone who had seen patterns repeat and evolve across eight decades. "It's changing you," she confirmed. "Opening pathways between human consciousness and mountain memory. Sarah discovered this before they silenced her."

I knelt, placing both palms flat against soil where my blood mixed with blue-green growth already pushing through contamination toward light. Connection flowed bidirectionally—not just human to stone but stone to human, communication older than language finding expression through cellular restructuring beyond scientific classification.

"I can hear it," I whispered. "Not words exactly. But intention.

Purpose. Memory flowing like water through channels I couldn't perceive before."

"The living stone speaks through many voices," Ruth said, her hand finding my shoulder. "Through Tsini's fire. Through Sarah's evidence. Through your altered blood. Through patterns that connect what corporate extraction tries to separate."

Around us, the federal investigation proceeded with institutional precision—evidence gathered, perimeters secured, statements recorded. Systems processing truth through channels they could control and categorize.

But beneath that official response, something else continued—water finding its level, truth rising through soil, memory flowing through blood that carried mountain knowledge in cellular structure altered beyond corporate calculation or federal classification.

Morrison approached, institutional purpose temporarily aligned with witnessed justice. "We need your statements," he said. "For the official record."

I looked to Ruth, who had testified before enough government bodies to recognize both the necessity and limitation of official documentation.

"We'll give you what your systems can process," she said with gentle recognition rather than dismissal. "The rest will flow through different channels."

As we followed Morrison toward waiting vehicles, I felt the mountain's presence not receding but transforming—spreading through water, through soil, through blood that carried memory beyond individual lifespan or institutional record.

And within me, radiation continued its strange work—not just destroying cells but creating pathways between human consciousness and geological memory, between individual lifespan and mountain time, between what systems calculated as separate but relationship recognized as unified.

"Will I survive this?" I asked Ruth as we descended the mound's slope toward vehicles that would carry us back to institutional processing of what had happened here.

"Not in the way their medicine measures survival," she answered with honesty shaped by eight decades witnessing cycles of death and continuation. "But neither will you end. The mountain doesn't forget those who protect it."

The strongbox waited in Ruth's truck where we had left it—evidence gathered by Sarah, protected by my radiation-damaged body, now flowing through channels corporate dams and federal classification couldn't fully contain.

Inside it lay proof of thirty-seven calculated deaths. Of corporate decision to poison a valley for mineral extraction. Of systemic valuing of profit above life. Important truth that needed institutional processing through courts and hearings and legal consequences.

But alongside that documented evidence flowed something else—truth carried through water that remembers its original channels despite dams and diversions. Through plants emerging from contaminated soil in patterns identical to basket designs woven for a thousand years. Through blood connecting human consciousness to mountain memory across generations corporate calculation had tried to sever.

"We should get your blood checked," Morrison said, noticing crimson still flowing freely from my nose, my ears, my eyes. "The radiation exposure—"

"Is doing exactly what it needs to do," I finished for him, certainty flowing through altered cells. "Some transformations can't be measured by institutional medicine."

As vehicles departed with Crowder in custody and evidence secured through multiple channels, I looked back at the mound—ancient sentinel in landscape corporate extraction had calculated as acceptable sacrifice for quarterly profit.

Blue-green plants continued their spiral expansion, following patterns Ruth had been weaving throughout her lifetime, creating living network that would carry truth through channels industrial contamination had inadvertently opened.

The mountain had remembered. And so had we.

Truth rising, like water, finding its level.

Chapter Five

THE MOUND AWAKENS

Corporate lights blazed against sacred stone. Metal against memory. Temporary against eternal.

The rain fell harder as we descended the ridge path, each drop carrying chemical signatures from Watershed's breach. I could taste cadmium and chromium on my lips, radiation-altered cells translating contamination into information. The mountain spoke through water, through stone, through blood now dripping from my nose in steady rhythm.

Ruth's ancient truck sat abandoned behind us, too visible against the ridge. Our footprints would wash away with rain. The federal agents in their black SUV would find nothing—just empty vehicle, maintenance road, storm washing evidence into channels they couldn't follow.

"There," I whispered, pointing toward the mound's western face where drainage tunnels from original construction created access their security grid ignored. "The water always finds paths through stone."

Ruth nodded, eyes tracking patrol patterns with the tactical assessment of woman who'd faced down federal agents at Wounded Knee, who'd blockaded uranium mines with her body, who'd carried indigenous resistance through channels designed to drown it. Her silver hair plastered against copper skin, turquoise earrings catching industrial light in defiant flashes.

"Six guards on rotation," she observed, counting intervals between movements. "Military training but private contract. No accountability to constitutional restrictions."

Below, the extraction site blazed with unnatural daylight. Excavators had already carved into the mound's eastern slope, core drilling equipment assembled with efficiency that spoke of deadline urgency. White-coated technicians moved between portable laboratory tents and collection stations, corporate scientists reducing sacred to sample.

The path narrowed as we descended, forcing single-file movement. My hands gripped roots and stones that felt alive beneath my touch, recognition flowing from mountain memory into radiation-altered cells. Each step connected me more deeply to forces corporate extraction had calculated as resource but existed as relationship.

Blood flowed freely now—not just from my nose but from ears, from eyes, from fingernails where capillaries had ruptured. Not just radiation damage but transformation, my body becoming conduit for communication between human consciousness and geological time.

"How much longer can you stand?" Ruth asked, the question pragmatic rather than fearful.

"Long enough," I answered, certainty flowing through altered pathways. "The radiation isn't just killing me. It's connecting me to something they're trying to extract."

Her eyes measured me—not with grandson's medical concern but with elder's recognition of transformation beyond institutional classification. "Sarah discovered this too, didn't she? Before they silenced her."

I nodded, wiping blood that immediately replaced itself. "Her last call, she was seeing patterns in the data no one else could. Connections between the living stone and human DNA. Specific markers in Cherokee bloodlines."

"That's why they want the valley emptied," Ruth concluded, pieces connecting with basket-weaver's precision. "Not just for mineral access. To remove the people whose blood recognizes what lies beneath."

We reached the forest's edge where darkness ended and industrial light began. Two hundred yards of exposed ground separated us from the drainage culvert I'd seen through altered perception. Two hundred yards where corporate security would spot us instantly.

Ruth's hand found mine, weathered fingers pressing something into my palm—a small cloth bundle, the weight familiar yet strange. "Your grandfather carried this at Oak Ridge," she said. "After the radiation changed him too."

I unwrapped the bundle to find smooth stone the size of water-worn creek pebble. Not ordinary rock but something that pulsed faintly with blue-green luminescence visible only to my altered senses.

"You've had a fragment of the living stone all along," I whispered, understanding crystallizing through pain.

"The mountain chooses its connections," she replied simply. "Your grandfather found this after three years handling uranium. Said it called to his poisoned blood. Kept him alive two decades past what doctors predicted."

The stone warmed against my skin, pulsing in rhythm that matched exactly the contaminated blood now flowing freely from my body. Not coincidence. Recognition. The radiation damage creating channels between human consciousness and geological memory.

"We need distraction to reach the culvert," I said, pocketing the fragment that hummed against my thigh like living presence. "Something to draw their attention."

Ruth's eyes moved to the secondary generator powering industrial lights on the mound's far side. "Fire always makes men look," she said, withdrawing the striker passed through generations since Tsini rescued flame from burning council house.

"That's three hundred yards away," I said. "You can't—"

"I didn't survive eight decades of federal policy by underestimating what my body can do," Ruth interrupted, calculation replacing conversation. "When the lights on the east side go, they'll reposition. That's our window."

Before I could protest, Ruth was moving, not toward the culvert but along the forest's edge, circling toward the generator's position.

Her body disappeared into shadows with precision born from decades evading surveillance at protests and blockades.

Left alone, I felt the radiation's transformation accelerating—cells changing structure not just from damage but from connection with the fragment in my pocket, with the larger deposit beneath the mound, with mountain memory flowing through stone into blood that recognized its patterns.

I could see differently now—not just visible spectrum but energy flowing through channels invisible to corporate instruments. The security grid glowed with artificial barriers, but between them flowed ancient pathways like underground rivers connecting supposedly separate territories.

Ten minutes passed. Then the eastern lights died with electrical scream that cut through rain percussion. Security personnel responded immediately, repositioning toward sudden darkness with tactical precision that left the western approach temporarily exposed.

Now.

I sprinted across open ground, each step sending daggers through radiation-altered nervous system. Blood trailed behind me, marking path like crimson breadcrumbs. Not stealth but speed became salvation—crossing exposed territory before security's sweep returned.

The culvert opening appeared before me, ancient stone arch incorporated into modern drainage. I slipped inside just as flashlight beams cut through rain where I'd stood seconds earlier.

Darkness embraced me, not as absence but as presence with its own consciousness. The tunnel smelled of wet stone and mineral-rich earth, water flowing around my ankles in patterns that spoke older truths than corporate extraction could measure or monitor.

I moved forward through passages that twisted according to water's wisdom rather than engineering efficiency. Above, boots thudded against packed earth. Voices called coordinates. Machines growled with hunger always unsatisfied.

The fragment in my pocket pulsed stronger with each step deeper, harmonizing with mountain memory flowing through stone into blood that recognized ancestral patterns. The connection growing clearer, less like translation and more like remembering language once known but temporarily forgotten.

The tunnel ended at maintenance grate that offered view of the mound's summit. There, beneath portable floodlights arranged like corporate crown, stood Lawrence Crowder himself—elegant in tailored suit despite rain and mud, examining core samples with the detached interest of someone calculating value against quarterly projections.

I pressed against the grate. It gave slightly, metal hasp loose against ancient stone that remembered what belonged and what didn't.

With gentle pressure, the grate swung open. Not locked at all, but secured by corporate assumption that separation meant security. That categorization equaled control.

I slipped onto the mound's surface, shadows gathering me into their protection. The fragment in my pocket pulled with increasing urgency, not just connection but communication with the larger deposit Crowder's equipment had exposed. The blue-green luminescence visible now even to unaltered perception, core samples glowing with living light that corporate instruments measured but couldn't understand.

I moved upward, body pressed against the mound's surface, blood marking sacred soil in pattern older than the Treaty of New Echota, older than America itself. Each step connecting me to Tsini, to Ruth, to generations who had protected this place against forces that calculated extraction above relationship.

At the summit, Crowder stood alone, rain plastering his expensive suit against corporate frame, his back to my approach as he studied blue-green material extracted from the mound's heart. The same blue-green that now pulsed through my radiation-altered blood.

"It's not yours to take," I said, my voice cutting through machine growl and rain percussion.

Crowder turned, surprise briefly crossing features trained to mask reaction. "Ms. Nighthawk," he said, corporate mask reasserting itself. "Your timing is inconvenient but not unexpected. Sarah showed similar determination before her unfortunate accident."

The casual reference to her murder sent rage burning through my veins. "Thirty-seven people dead. A valley poisoned for generations. A sacred site violated. All for what's in your hand."

Crowder's smile contained no warmth, only calculation. "Progress requires difficult decisions. Resources vital to national security often demand extraction under suboptimal conditions."

"You call thirty-seven deaths 'suboptimal conditions'?" Blood ran freely down my chin now, marking ground between us in patterns my altered vision recognized as identical to the living stone's crystalline structure.

His eyes tracked the crimson path, scientific curiosity momentarily overcoming corporate caution. "Your radiation badge from the lab suggests you shouldn't be alive," he observed. "Yet here you are, hemorrhaging but conscious. Fascinating."

"You deliberately exposed Sarah to radiation," I said, pieces connecting through altered perception. "Not just to silence her, but to study how it interacted with her contact with these samples."

"Dr. Chen was a promising researcher who unfortunately lost perspective on the larger mission." Crowder's tone suggested administrative regret rather than human recognition. "Her exposure provided valuable data on how the material interacts with altered cellular structures. Data your current condition is enhancing considerably."

The fragment in my pocket burned against my thigh, responding to both the core sample in Crowder's hand and the blood now flowing freely from my body. Connection forming triangle that corporate instruments could measure but couldn't comprehend.

"The material beneath this mound represents the largest deposit of non-terrestrial rare earth elements ever discovered," Crowder continued, scientific fascination competing with corporate containment. "Elements with properties that respond to specific genetic markers." His eyes measured me like core sample. "Cherokee markers."

The revelation landed like physical blow. Not just minerals. Not just sacred land. Something the mountain had protected for centuries because it responded to bloodlines connected to this specific place.

"That's why you calculated our deaths as acceptable," I said, understanding crystallizing through pain. "You needed the reservation empty. Needed Cherokee bloodlines removed from proximity to the living stone."

"Indigenous land claims are temporary inconveniences in resource development timelines," Crowder confirmed, repeating what he'd told Sarah weeks before her death. "The flood created necessary legal circumstances for federal disaster acquisition. Once declared a contamination zone, this entire valley falls under emergency management protocols—circumventing tribal sovereignty entirely."

Rain intensified around us, each drop carrying chemical signatures from the retention pond breach, the water itself testifying to deliberate contamination. Lightning forked across cloud-heavy sky, illuminating the excavation site in stark flashes—machinery assembled with military efficiency, core samples stored in specialized containers, technicians documenting extraction with precision that served corporate purpose.

"The evidence is already public," I said, stalling while the fragment in my pocket communicated with blood and stone in dance invisible to corporate perception. "Sarah's documentation of the deliberate breach. The falsified safety reports. Your signature on the cost-benefit analysis calculating thirty-sevendeaths against mineral access."

Crowder's expression remained unmoved, corporate certainty undisturbed. "Evidence requires functioning legal system to have meaning," he countered smoothly. "One call from the Defense Department citing critical resource needs, and everything becomes classified. Unreviewable. Inadmissible."

"The tribal newspaper already published—"

"A charming publication with limited distribution and less credibility," he interrupted. "Digital evidence can be discredited. Witnesses intimidated. The narrative controlled."

As he spoke, the blue-green material in his hand pulsed stronger, energy responding to our conversation through channels corporate instruments couldn't detect but my radiation-altered blood perceived with increasing clarity.

"You've analyzed the material composition," I said, voice steady despite blood now flowing from eyes like ceremonial tears. "But have you considered its consciousness?"

Crowder's expression shifted from corporate certainty to scientific caution. "Consciousness is not a property of geological formations."

"Neither is blue-green luminescence that responds to genetic markers," I countered. "Neither is molecular restructuring that communicates across separate samples. Neither is radiation resistance that transforms cellular damage into perceptual pathways."

The ground trembled slightly. Not earthquake but recognition. The mountain listening through stone older than human language.

Around us, scientists looked up from instruments suddenly registering anomalous data. Security personnel touched earpieces receiving concerning reports. Equipment faltered, readings spiked, communications stuttered.

Crowder's hand tightened around the core sample, corporate control battling forces beyond quarterly projection. "Whatever you think is happening, Ms. Nighthawk, it changes nothing. This material is worth trillions. Worth thirty-seven deaths. Worth an entire contaminated valley."

I withdrew the fragment from my pocket, the living stone now glowing with blue-green light visible even through falling rain. "And worth whatever happens to you when the mountain remembers what men like you have always forgotten."

As the words left my lips, the fragment flared with sudden intensity —light connecting it to the core sample in Crowder's hand, to similar pieces being studied in portable labs around the mound, to the larger deposit still embedded in sacred soil. Not separate elements but unified network, communication flowing through channels corporate extraction had inadvertently activated.

Crowder stared at the fragment, corporate calculation giving way to scientific alarm. "Where did you get that?"

"From ancestors who recognized relationship isn't something you extract." I let blood from my palm drip directly onto the fragment, completing connection that mountain memory had prepared through generations. "It's something you protect."

The effect was immediate and undeniable. The fragment's blue-green light intensified, spreading upward along my arm, across my torso, illuminating blood vessels in patterns that matched exactly the crystalline structure of the living stone itself.

Around us, similar illumination spread through the excavation site —core samples glowing in laboratory containment, testing equipment registering impossible energy signatures, the ground itself beginning to pulse with light that emerged from between soil particles like living presence awakening from sleep.

"What have you done?" Crowder demanded, the core sample in his hand now burning with intensity that caused him to drop it. Unlike me, his blood shared no relationship with what it contained. His DNA recognized no ancestral patterns flowing through stone.

"I haven't done anything," I answered truthfully. "The mountain is remembering. The pattern is changing."

A security officer approached, radio crackling with static that formed sounds in no human language. "Sir, we're getting unusual readings from all sample sites. The material is becoming unstable."

"Implement containment protocols," Crowder ordered, voice steady but eyes revealing fractures in corporate certainty. "Full extraction team to primary deposit immediately."

But the blue-green light continued spreading, moving from fragments to soil to air itself, creating network visible to human perception but operating through principles corporate science couldn't classify or control.

The ground beneath us shuddered—not collapse but awakening. Fissures opened in perfect spiral patterns that matched exactly the designs Ruth wove into river cane baskets, that appeared in Cherokee pottery fragments thousands of years old, that flowed through my radiation-altered blood in molecular restructuring beyond scientific classification.

Scientists backed away from instruments that crossed from controlled experiment to witnessed phenomenon beyond institutional categorization. Security personnel raised weapons against threat they couldn't target or contain. Extraction equipment stood idle as operators fled illumination spreading across the mound's surface.

And still I stood at the center, blood marking patterns on stone that had witnessed centuries of ceremony, of protection, of relationship corporate calculation could never understand.

"It's over, Crowder," I said, voice carrying through rain fallen suddenly silent, through machines grown suddenly still, through corporate certainty suddenly irrelevant.

"Nothing's over," he insisted, though conviction had drained from his tone, leaving only man confronting forces his quarterly reports couldn't accommodate. "The legal machinery is already in motion. The federal classification order signed. The extraction permits secured."

The blue-green light intensified around us, creating illumination that passed through human tissue as if it didn't exist, revealing connections invisible to corporate perception but clear to blood that carried mountain memory.

Another, deeper tremor passed through the mound—energy shifting states beneath our feet, changing relationship between elements corporate extraction had calculated as separate but the living stone recognized as unified.

From the maintenance tunnel emerged Ruth, her physical presence bringing ancestral authority to mountain awakening. She walked directly toward us, silver hair catching blue-green light like living fire, turquoise earrings reflecting illumination that connected sky to stone.

"The pattern never just repeats," she said, voice carrying through the suddenly attentive air. "It evolves."

A final, more powerful tremor opened chasm at the mound's very center—not destruction but emergence, as if something dormant now awakened. Blue-green light shot upward in column that pierced rain clouds, visible for miles across darkened valley.

The light had texture—not just illumination but substance. It carried scent like cedar after rain, like stone warmed by summer sun, like blood carrying memory through generations. It sounded like water finding its level, like branches creaking with winter ice, like heartbeats synchronized across centuries.

Watershed's personnel fled in disorganized retreat—corporate security abandoning posts, scientists leaving equipment, technicians forgetting samples in haste to escape forces their instruments could measure but couldn't comprehend.

Only Crowder remained, corporate identity crumbling as individual confronted energies beyond extraction's understanding. "What is this?" he asked, voice stripped of authority, revealing only man witnessing truth his systems couldn't process.

"The mountain remembering what you tried to extract," I answered, blood flowing freely into sacred soil but pain transforming into something else—not absence but expansion, consciousness extending beyond individual boundaries into networks older than human settlement.

The blue-green light began to recede, drawing back into the mound, into the soil, into the water running through channels older than human settlement. But where it passed, it left change—not just in illumination but in relationship between elements corporate extraction had categorized as separate but the mountain recognized as unified.

"It's communicating," Crowder whispered, scientific curiosity momentarily overcoming corporate failure. "A non-organic consciousness using electromagnetic frequency as transmission medium."

"Not communicating," Ruth corrected. "Remembering. Like water remembers its original channels despite dams and diversions."

The light continued its retreat, concentration shifting from atmospheric dispersion to focused presence in the mound itself. The fissures remained—spiral patterns that matched exactly basket designs woven for thousand years, pathways through which water would now flow, carrying memory beyond individual perception or corporate containment.

As darkness returned, Crowder stood abandoned by extraction machinery, by security forces, by scientific certainty that had calculated indigenous lives as acceptable losses against quarterly profit. The rain resumed, washing blood and mud down the mound's slopes in rivulets that followed newly formed channels.

"This evidence will never reach court," he insisted, final attempt to assert corporate patterns that had always worked before. "The classification order—"

"Is irrelevant," I interrupted, blood still flowing but pain transformed into clarity beyond institutional medicine's ability to measure. "The evidence isn't just documents and testimonies. It's flowing through channels your systems can't control. Through water. Through soil. Through blood that carries mountain memory across generations corporate calculation tried to sever."

Ruth's hand found mine, connection flowing between us—grandmother to granddaughter, past to present, pattern recognized to pattern transformed. "Truth doesn't need human permission to rise," she said simply.

The sound of vehicles approaching broke the moment—not corporate security returning but tribal police arriving alongside federal agents, their lights cutting through rain with red and blue urgency.

Morrison emerged first, weapon drawn and federal authority temporarily aligned with witnessed justice. "Lawrence Crowder," he announced, "you're under arrest for environmental terrorism, negligent homicide, and conspiracy to violate tribal sovereignty."

Crowder's shoulders sagged imperceptibly—not surrender but recognition that systems he'd navigated with corporate precision had encountered forces beyond their classification or control. "This material is vital to national security," he said, institutional reflex asserting itself even in defeat. "The Defense Department will intervene."

"Perhaps," Morrison acknowledged, securing restraints around corporate wrists. "But some truths flow through channels even the Pentagon can't dam."

As they led Crowder toward waiting vehicles, Ruth and I remained on the mound's summit, watching federal response organize itself with institutional efficiency—evidence secured, perimeters established, statements recorded. Systems processing through channels they understood while missing the deeper transformation flowing beneath visible surface.

"Look," Ruth said, pointing toward the soil where Crowder's team had begun extraction. From disturbed earth, tiny blue-green shoots emerged—plants unlike any botanical classification, following spiral patterns identical to Ruth's basket designs. This was not random growth but deliberate communication, the mountain's memory finding new expression through channels corporate extraction had inadvertently opened.

My blood continued flowing, marking sacred ground with patterns the living stone recognized. But the pain had receded, replaced by perception beyond individual boundaries—consciousness expanding through networks radiation damage had opened between human awareness and geological memory.

"The living stone was never just mineral deposit," I said, understanding flowing through altered cells. "It's communication medium. Bridge between human and mountain consciousness."

Ruth nodded, her eight decades witnessing cycles of exploitation and resistance crystallizing into recognition beyond institutional classification. "The pattern never just repeats," she repeated, hand sweeping toward blue-green growth already transforming contaminated soil. "It evolves."

Mordi appeared from tribal police vehicles, medical bag in hand, his steps accelerating when he saw blood saturating my clothing. "You need to be in a hospital," he insisted, professional assessment overriding personal connection. "The radiation damage—"

"Isn't just destroying," I finished for him, certainty flowing through altered pathways. "It's transforming. Creating channels between my consciousness and the living stone's network." I pointed toward blood that continued flowing freely yet caused no weakness, no dizziness, no diminishment of awareness. "Look at me, Mordi. Really look. Do I present as someone experiencing lethal radiation poisoning?"

His physician's eyes cataloged symptoms that contradicted medical expectation—hemorrhaging without shock, cellular damage without deteriorating function, radiation exposure without expected collapse. "Something's happening beyond medical classification," he acknowledged finally. "But that doesn't mean it isn't killing you, just differently."

"Maybe death itself is just transition between states of consciousness," Ruth suggested, basket-weaver's philosophy cutting through medical certainty with insight shaped by eight decades witnessing cycles of ending and beginning. "Maybe the mountain is teaching her different ways to continue."

Federal agents swarmed the excavation site, securing samples with hazardous materials protocols and documenting equipment with evidence processing precision. Morrison approached, institutional duty temporarily aligned with witnessed justice but uncertainty written across features trained to mask reaction.

"The Defense Department is already claiming jurisdiction," he informed us, voice lowered despite rain that masked conversation. "Classification orders are being prepared. This will disappear into federal secrecy by morning."

Ruth's laugh carried wisdom earned through eight decades of watching systems rise and fall while the mountain remained. "They can claim jurisdiction over land and take samples into laboratories," she said. "But the living stone is already spreading through channels they can't monitor or control." Her hand swept toward blue-green plants emerging from the soil in perfect spiral patterns. "The mountain has found a new voice. One that speaks without human permission."

As federal agents secured the site and tribal police established protective boundaries, I knelt to touch soil where my blood mixed with living stone in patterns that institutional science couldn't classify. The connection flowed bidirectionally—not just human to mountain but mountain to human, communication older than language finding expression through cellular restructuring beyond medical categorization.

"I can hear it," I whispered, perception extending beyond individual boundaries. "Not words exactly. But intention. Purpose. Memory flowing like water through channels opened by radiation."

"The mountain speaks through many voices," Ruth said, hand finding my shoulder. "Through Tsini's fire. Through Sarah's evidence. Through your altered blood. Through patterns that connect what corporate extraction tries to separate."

"Will you survive this?" Morrison asked directly, human concern momentarily overriding institutional containment.

I looked to Ruth, who had witnessed lifetimes begin and end while patterns continued beyond individual existence. "Not in the form medicine measures," I answered honestly echoing Ruth's earlier assessment. "But neither will I end. The mountain doesn't forget those who protect it."

As we descended the mound toward waiting vehicles, I felt transformation accelerating through altered cells—radiation damage creating not destruction but communication channels between human consciousness and geological memory. The blue-green growth continued spreading across soil corporate models had classified as permanently contaminated, following patterns identical to basket designs Ruth had woven throughout her lifetime.

"The legal investigation will continue," Morrison said, institutional purpose reasserting itself as we reached tribal police vehicles. "Criminal charges against Crowder and corporate executives. Environmental remediation orders. Federal oversight of contamination zone."

Important processes that would create consequences through human systems designed to balance extraction against impact. Necessary justice operating through channels that corporate power recognized and sometimes respected.

But alongside those institutional responses flowed something else—truth carried through water that remembered its original channels despite dams and diversions. Through plants emerging from contaminated soil in patterns identical to basket designs woven for thousand years. Through blood connecting human consciousness to geological memory across generations corporate calculation had tried to sever.

"Get some rest," Morrison advised as we prepared to leave. "Tomorrow will bring federal investigators, media inquiries, legal proceedings."

"Tomorrow will bring whatever the mountain remembers," Ruth corrected gently. "Your systems will process what they can comprehend. The rest will flow through different channels."

As the federal agents departed with Crowder in custody and evidence secured, I looked back at the mound—ancient sentinel in landscape corporate extraction had calculated as acceptable sacrifice for quarterly profit. Blue-green plants continued their spiral expansion, following patterns Ruth had been weaving throughout her lifetime, creating a living network that would carry truth through channels industrial contamination had inadvertently opened.

"Did we win?" I asked Ruth as we drove toward thereservation's boundaries, where tribal medicine would be able to monitor a transformation beyond institutional classification.

Her smile contained wisdom earned through eight decades spent-watching cycles of exploitation and resistance, destruction and creation, patterns that repeat but constantly evolve. "Victory isn't what your generation imagines," she said. "It is not triumph that ends struggle but continuation that outlasts systems designed to contain it."

The moon emerged from storm clouds, illuminating a valley forever changed but not destroyed. Damaged but not defeated. Poisoned but now finding healing through channels corporate models had never calculated, federal agencies couldn't classify, extraction technologies couldn't control.

The mountain remembered. And so had we.

Truth rising, like water, finding its level.

Chapter Six

TOXIC WATERS

Jamie's blood dripped onto sacred ground. Not metaphorical blood—actual red droplets seeping into soil that had absorbed Cherokee suffering for centuries. The same soil that now sprouted blue-green plants where nothing should grow.

It had been three days since the mound had awakened. Three days since federal agents swarmed the valley with instruments that measured but couldn't comprehend. Three days of media reports struggling to categorize events through frameworks too limited to contain them. Three days of my body continuing its strange transformation—blood still flowing but pain replaced by perception extending beyond individual boundaries.

Morrison stood over Jamie's kneeling form. "Tell me who authorized the third retention pond breach," he demanded, institutional authority momentarily aligned with witnessed justice.

Jamie's eyes found mine across the distance, pleading not for forgiveness but understanding. His face carried fresh bruises—cheekbone darkening into storm clouds, lip split like a valley suffering corporate division. "You don't understand what you've awakened," he said, words directed at me rather than the agent hovering above him.

"I found him at the north retention pond," Morrison explained, addressing Ruth and me while maintaining tactical vigilance. "He was placing charges at critical stress points. My team intervened before detonation."

The north retention pond. The last of the ponds and the largest of the three. The one directly above the reservation's main residential area.

"Another engineered flood," I said, the realization coming with certainty. "Another 'acceptable loss' calculation?"

Jamie shook his head, blood from his split lip spotting the blue-green plants that had proliferated since the mound's awakening. "Not like before," he insisted. "Different purpose. Different command structure."

"Whose purpose?" Morrison pressed, federal interrogation techniques sharpening his questions. "Watershed Security? Military contractors? Foreign interests?"

Rain began falling, gentle at first but rapidly intensifying, as if the mountain coordinated all elements in response to presentthreats. Water carried information my altered cells could read—chemical signatures from the retention pond, microscopic particles from explosives Jamie's team had attempted to place, hormones from human bodies calculating further destruction.

"They're afraid of what's growing," Jamie said, eyes tracking the blue-green plants spreading across the valley in patterns identical to Ruth's basket designs. "Afraid of what they can't control. The Defense Department classified everything after the mound incident. Ordered all samples be contained and all evidence suppressed."

Ruth's fingers moved in basket-weaving patterns, creating invisible structure to hold emerging truth. "But the living stone is spreading beyond their containment," she observed. "Following channels their instruments can't track."

Jamie nodded, resignation replacing resistance. "That's why they sent us. The Pentagon's assessment concluded that complete irradiation of the valley is the only guaranteed containment method. The pond breach would allow them to introduce radioactive material under the guise of disaster response."

"They want to poison the entire valley?" Morrison's federal certainty cracked visibly. "That's thirty thousand acres, including tribal lands protected by treaty."

"Treaties mean nothing against national security directives," Ruth said dryly. "That pattern hasn't changed since 1819."

The rain intensified further, water connecting sky to earth in sheets that obscured distant mountains. Not random precipitation but deliberate communication, the weather itself responding to the threat against the living network now spreading throughout the valley.

"When was the breach scheduled to happen?" I asked Jamie directly, blood from my eyes mixing with rainfall to create rivulets down my face like ceremonial paint.

"Tonight at 11 p.m." His eyes held mine with desperate intensity. "I came to warn you. That's why I let Morrison catch me. The infiltration team is still moving forward—four operatives with military-grade explosives."

The implications crystallized with terrible clarity. Another flood, but carrying intentional radiation rather than industrial byproduct. Another "Act of God" concealing corporate and government collaboration. Another calculation of indigenous lives as acceptable sacrifice for systems threatened by forces they couldn't control.

"We need to evacuate the reservation," Morrison said immediately, federal emergency protocols engaging. "I'll contact tribal police and—"

"No," I interrupted, certainty flowing through altered pathways. "That's what they want. The reservation empty so they can implement complete contamination without witnesses."

Ruth nodded in agreement with my assessment. "If we evacuate, they'll have free access. If we stay, they'll be forced to explain mass casualties of people who were never officially threatened."

"Then we stop the breach," Morrison insisted, focusing on immediate threat containment.

"We do more than that," I countered. "We change the pattern completely."

Rain continued falling with increasing deliberation, drops carrying information between sky and soil, human and mountain, memory and potential. My altered perception could read these communications now—not as translation but as direct awareness, consciousness extending beyond individual boundaries into networks older than human settlement.

"The retention pond is already failing," I said, knowledge flowing through pathways radiation had opened between my cells and the living stone. "The recent tremors from the mound's awakening created stress fractures throughout the northern basin. That's why they selected it for their operation—they can blame natural forces for what they plan to trigger artificially."

Morrison's radio crackled with static—federal communications struggling against atmospheric conditions the mountain itself was generating. "Control teams are reporting unusual weather patterns throughout the valley," a voice reported through electronic distortion. "Localized precipitation exceeding meteorological predictions by 400 percent. Communication systems experiencing unexplained disruption."

Not technical malfunction but deliberate interference, the mountain coordinating defense of its own.

"We need to move now," I said, plans formulating not through individual strategy but through connection with networks flowing through soil, through water, through air itself. "Not just to stop the breach but to redirect it."

"Redirect a flood?" Morrison's federal skepticism battled with witnessed phenomena his systems couldn't classify. "That's not tactically viable."

"Water remembers its original channels," Ruth said, weathered hands moving in patterns that mapped flow through resistance. "Before dams and concrete and corporate restructuring, this valley had natural defenses against flooding. Channels the mountain carved over millennia to direct water away from residential areas."

I nodded, blood and rain mixing on my face as perception extended beyond individual boundaries. "The old streambeds. The pathways that existed before the Army Corps rerouted the watershed in 1956. They're still there beneath modern development."

"And how exactly do we convince several million gallons of water to follow your ancestral channel?" Morrison asked, federal pragmatism struggling against concepts beyond institutional classification.

"We don't convince the water," I answered, certainty flowing through me. "We remind it."

Jamie looked up from his kneeling position, scientific understanding battling corporate conditioning. "The blue-green growth," he said, recognition dawning across his bruised features. "It's following those original waterways, isn't it? Creating living channels the flood will recognize."

The pattern connected in ways federal instruments could measure, but corporate models couldn't predict. The living stone spoke not just through individual fragments but through networks extending throughout the valley, preparing defenses against threats its consciousness had anticipated before human instruments detected them.

"Can you stand?" I asked Jamie directly.

Morrison stepped between us, federal authority reasserting itself. "He stays in custody. After what he planned to do—"

"He's betraying his handlers to warn us," I interrupted. "And we need his knowledge of their operational details."

For a moment, Morrison's institutional training battled withreality —federal protocols demanding containment while present circumstances required adaptation. Finally, he nodded, pragmatism overriding procedure. "He remains restrained and under my direct supervision."

I helped Jamie to his feet, feeling the living stone's energy flow through my hand into his—not just physical support but a connection beyond individual boundaries. The blue-green plants beneath us responded, tendrils curling toward our feet like recognition.

"Four insertion teams approaching from different vectors," Jamie explained once vertical, blood still dripping from his split lip onto soil that absorbed it with deliberate purpose. "Using remnant drainage tunnels from original construction. They'll place synchronized charges at stress points I helped identify."

"And you know these access points?" Ruth asked, strategic assessment engaging.

"I mapped them myself," Jamie admitted, shame and determination wrestling across his features. "Standard protocol for extraction site security."

"Then that's our advantage," I said, plans crystallizing through networks flowing between human strategy and mountain memory. "Morrison's team intercepts the infiltration units while we prepare the channels for redirection."

"We'll need time," Ruth observed, eight decades of resistance teaching her that timing determined success more than force. "And they'll have communication equipment our tribal police can't match."

"The mountain will handle communications," I said with certainty beyond evidence, feeling atmospheric changes carrying information between elements corporate models calculated as separate but the living stone recognized as unified. "Your federal channels are already degrading in this storm," I told Morrison. "Theirs will too."

Morrison studied me with institutional assessment battling witnessed phenomena—the blood still flowing from my eyes, nose, and ears without causing expected physical deterioration, the blue-green plants responding to my presence, the storm intensifying with precision beyond meteorological prediction.

"What's happening to you?" he asked finally, human question penetrating federal facade. "The radiation damage—"

"Is transformation, not destruction," Ruth answered for me, her hand finding my shoulder with connection flowing between generations. "The mountain speaks through many voices. Through Tsini's fire. Through Sarah's evidence. Through Esther's altered blood."

The rain continued with heightened intensity, storm creating conditions that would mask our movements while hampering infiltration teams approaching with technological advantage but without relationship to the land they sought to flood.

"Six hours until their planned detonation," Morrison calculated, federal precision measuring limited time against necessary action. "How do we coordinate across multiple sites with communications compromised?"

Ruth smiled. "The same way our people have always communicated when federal channels weren't available to us," she said, drawing a small leather pouch from jacket pocket. "With methods your systems dismissed as primitive while we preserved their effectiveness."

Inside the pouch nestled smooth stones in various colors—not arandom collection but a deliberate communication system older than the telegraph or radio. "River code," she explained, selecting stones with practiced precision. "Patterns arranged at key locations that carry specific meanings to those who know how to read them."

I nodded, ancestral knowledge connecting with present necessity. "The tribal police will understand without electronic communication. Place the patterns at trail junctions and water crossings, and our people will mobilize."

"That still leaves the infiltration teams to manage," Morrison said, federal training focusing on tactical containment.

"You handle your systems, Agent Morrison," Ruth replied, already beginning to place stones in patterns that would carry warnings through networks federal instruments couldn't monitor. "The mountain will handle its own."

Plans crystallized with the precision born from urgency. Morrison would deploy his agents to intercept the infiltration teams approaching with explosives. Ruth would activate tribal communication networks to mobilize community response. Jamie would identify access points and tactical vulnerabilities from inside knowledge. I would connect with the living stone's network to ensure water remembered its original channels when the breach occurred.

As we separated to address our separate tasks, Jamie caught my arm, his eyes carrying regret beyond words. "I didn't know what would happen when I joined Watershed," he said quietly. "I thought it was just another extraction operation with negativeenvironmental impact."

"And when you discovered the truth?"

His gaze dropped to blue-green plants that curled around his feet with an awareness that transcended normal botanical behavior. "I should have acted sooner," he acknowledged. "When they went after Sarah, I should have done more."

"Inaction is rooted in fear. Fear of taking the wrong action. Fear of making the wrong choice," I replied, thinking of ancestors who chose to follow water's path through systems designed to eliminate them.

"But water, it remembers its channels despite dams and diversions. It stays true to itself."

The storm continued with deliberate intensity as we moved toward separate tasks—Ruth placing stone patterns that would mobilize tribal response, Morrison coordinating federal interception of infiltration teams, and Jamie sharing the access points his former colleagues would use to approach the retention pond.

I walked alone toward the northern edge of the reservation,where the living channel the blue-green plants had created wasmost concentrated. My body moved with strange grace despite blood still flowing from various orifices—the transformationcontinued with radiation damage creating pathways between human consciousness and geological memory.

The reservation center lay directly below the north retention pond, three hundred homes inhabited by elders, families, and children who carried Cherokee bloodlines through generations.If the infiltration teams succeeded, these homes and people would disappear beneath a flood carrying deliberate radiation rather than just industrial byproduct.

But unlike previous threats, the mountain was now awake. The living stone's network had spread throughout the valley. The blue-green plants formed living channels that followed exactly the waterways that had existed before the Army Corps rerouting, before concrete channelization, before corporate restructuring of natural hydrology.

I reached the northern boundary where the plants grew most concentrated. Kneeling, I placed both palms flat against the earth, feeling the pulse of consciousness within the soil.

"Show me," I whispered, blood from my eyes, nose, and ears mixing with rain to create patterns on soil that matched exactly the living stone's crystalline structure. "Show me the original channels."

Connection formed instantly—not translation but direct awareness, consciousness extending beyond individual boundaries into networks older than human settlement. I could see beneath visible surfaces to waterways that had existed for millennia before corporate models calculated them as inefficient and rerouted their flow.

The blue-green plants were creating living channels that would guide water back to these original pathways—not through engineering but through relationship, reminding liquid consciousness of routes carved through stone over geological timeframes. When the flood came, whether through natural failure or detonated charges, it would follow these reestablished connections rather than corporate predictions.

As night fell, the storm intensified further, rain creating conditions that would both hide our preparations and hamper infiltration teams approaching with destructive purpose. Lightning flashed, illuminating the valley in stroboscopic revelation that exposed not just the physical landscape but theenergetic connections flowing between supposedly separate elements.

My phone vibrated—Morrison coordinating despite communications degrading with each passing hour. "Two teams intercepted," the text read through electronic distortion. "Two still at large. Explosives confirmed. Expected at target by 10p.m."

An hour before scheduled detonation. An hour to ensure water remembered its original channels when the dam failed.

I continued working with the blue-green growth, my hands guiding tendrils into patterns that matched precisely the designs Ruth wove into river cane baskets, that appeared in Cherokee pottery fragments thousands of years old, that flowed through my radiation-altered blood in molecular restructuring beyond scientific classification.

The plants responded to my touch with an awareness that transcended normal botanical behavior, tendrils reaching toward my blood-smeared fingers in recognition. Not controlling but cooperating, human consciousness and the living stone's network.

At 9:30 p.m., Ruth arrived with tribal elders who carried knowledge passed down through generations despite federal policies designed to erase it. They surrounded the living channels I'd been establishing, their voices raised in songs federal education had failed to extinguish, their bodies moving in patterns corporate anthropology had classified as ceremonial but existed as practical guidance of energy through intentional pathways.

"The stones are placed," Ruth informed me, her hands never

pausing in their basket-weaving motions. "Our people are securing homes and gathering at the community center. Morrison's teams have intercepted two more operatives, but at least one got through."

"One is enough," I acknowledged, blood streaming freely but consciousness clearer than at any time since the radiation transformation began. "They only need a single detonation to trigger a chain reaction through existing stress fractures."

The elders continued singing, their voices merging with rain percussion and thunder punctuation to create an acoustic environment that carried information between human awareness and geological memory. Not symbolic ritual but practical technology operating through principles corporate science couldn't classify or control.

At 9:45, Jamie arrived with Morrison, both men drenched from the storm that seemed to intensify with each passing minute. "Final operative spotted approaching northwest drainage tunnel," Morrison reported, federal precision clipped by urgency. "My team lost him in the storm. Communications completely compromised now."

Jamie studied the living channels we'd established. "You're creating an alternative drainage network," he realized, engineering training recognizing patterns beneath apparent randomness. "Hydrological redirection through botanical conductive paths."

"Not creating," Ruth corrected gently. "Remembering. The water knows where it belongs. We're just removing barriers to that flow."

At 9:55, a stillness settled over the valley—the last member of the infiltration team had reached one of the retention pond's structural weak points. The blue-green plants responded to the threat immediately, tendrils extending with accelerated growth, creating connections that solidified living channels in anticipation of approaching flood.

"Five minutes," Morrison calculated, federal training focusing on immediate threat containment. "Should we attempt final evacuation?"

"No time," Ruth assessed, strategic patience shaped by eight decades confronting systems of power. "And unnecessary if the channels hold."

At 9:59, lightning struck the retention pond's northern edge with precision beyond meteorological probability. Not random electrical discharge but deliberate communication, the mountain coordinating all elements in defense of its own memory. Thunder shook the valley with a physical force that resonated through soil, through water, and through blood that carried ancestral recognition.

At 10:00 p.m. exactly, an explosion rumbled burst through the calm—man-made destruction meeting mountain-made response. The retention pond's concrete wall fractured along the stress lines Jamie had identified, water beginning its release with a mathematical certainty corporate engineers could calculate, but on a path they couldn't predict.

The sound that followed defied institutional description—not just concrete failing or water rushing but consciousness awakening, the mountain speaking through the unified living stone.

"It's coming," Ruth said, fingers never pausing in their weaving despite invisible materials. "Now we see if the mountain remembers its own paths."

The flood approached with unstoppable momentum, millions of gallons released in a cascading torrent that corporate models predicted would scour the reservation clean in fifteen devastating minutes. Water carrying deliberate contamination—a final solution to a problem their containment couldn't resolve.

However, as the leading edge reached the zone where blue-green plants had established living channels, the water slowed andthen divided, following patterns invisible to satellite imagery but clear to the consciousness that recognized the memory of the land.

"Look," Jamie breathed, engineering training confronting phenomena his education couldn't classify. "It's diverting along the growth patterns. Following botanical guidance like adaptive nanotechnology."

Not technology but relationship—water remembering paths carved through stone over geological timeframes, responding to living channels established by the stone's network.

"It's working," Morrison said, federal assessment unable to mask genuine wonder. "The water is . . . listening to your plants?"

"Not listening," Ruth corrected. "Remembering. Water carries its own consciousness that corporate channelization temporarily redirected but never truly controlled."

The flood continued its division, following living networks that guided it away from human settlement toward natural collection basins that had existed before Army Corps intervention. Not harmless—trees still fell, erosion still occurred, natural landscape was still transformed by water's powerful passage—but without the human casualties that corporate models had calculated as acceptable losses.

I stood at the network's nexus point, blood flowing freely into living channels that carried communication between human consciousness and geological memory. Through radiation-altered perception, I could see beyond physical movement to information exchange occurring between water molecules and plant cells, between soil microbes and stone particles, between elements corporate science had categorized as separate but mountain memory recognized as unified.

"It's not just diverting the water," I said, understanding flowing through altered pathways. "It's extracting the radiation they introduced. The living stone is drawing contamination into itself, transforming molecular structure to neutralize its application."

Jamie stared at blue-green plants now glowing faintly as they absorbed radiation from the diverted water, his scientific training struggling to comprehend the phenomena before him. "It's using contamination as an energy source," he realized. "Converting radiation into biological accelerant for its own expansion."

The very weapon government tacticians had deployed against the living stone's network was now fueling its growth.

For thirty minutes, we stood witness as the flood continued its division and diversion, following living channels established through cooperation between human guidance and mountain memory. When the retention pond finally emptied, its toxic contents were distributed through a watershed network that neutralized contamination while preserving human settlement.Silence returned to the valley, broken only by steady rain that seemed to wash residual energy back into the soil from which it had emerged.

"I need to check the community center," Ruth said, practical concern overriding philosophical observation. "Some flooding likely reached outlying structures."

"My team will coordinate damage assessment," Morrison added, calling on his federal response protocols despite witnessingphenomena his systems couldn't classify. "And locate remaining infiltration operatives if they survived their own operation."

They departed toward the reservation center, leaving Jamie and me alone with a living network that continued pulsing with subtle luminescence—the blue-green plants processing radiation they had extracted from the flood, transforming contamination into energy that would fuel further growth beyond corporate containment or federal monitoring.

"I never understood what Watershed was really extracting," Jamie said, watching plants respond to residual water with movement that suggested consciousness beyond botanical classification. "I thought it was just rare earth minerals with unusual properties. Never imagined a living network connecting human bloodlines to geological formations."

"That's why their models always miscalculated," I replied, blood still flowing but pain replaced by perception extending beyond human boundaries. "They measured separate components without recognizing relationship as a fundamental principle rather than an exploitable resource."

Jamie's eyes tracked blood streaming from my eyes, nose, ears. "Will you survive this transformation? The radiation damage—"

"Is becoming something else," I finished for him, certainty flowing through altered pathways. "Not destruction but communication, neural networks restructuring to allow awareness beyond individual boundaries." I touched a blue-green plant that curled around my fingers with recognition beyond botanical classification. "I'm becoming a translator between human consciousness and geological memory."

"At what cost?" he pressed, engineering precision seeking measurable outcomes.

"Individual lifespan versus expanded awareness," I answered honestly. "This body will likely fail within a year, but myconsciousness will continue through the networks the mountain is establishing across watersheds and bloodlines."

His scientific skepticism battled with witnessed phenomena—the flood's clear response to living channels, the plants' obvious absorption

of radiation, the mountain's deliberate coordination of storm conditions that had hampered infiltration operations while supporting
indigenous defense.

"What happens now?" he asked finally. "The Pentagon won't simply
abandon their containment objectives. They'll develop new
approaches, deploy different technologies, calculate alternative
strategies."

"And the mountain will respond through channels they can't
control," I said, watching blue-green growth continuing its expansion
through soil once poisoned but now healing through a network none
could have imagined. "Water finds its level. Truth rises through
barriers designed to contain it. Memory flows through channels that
connect what extraction tries to separate."

Dawn approached with gentle illumination, revealing a valley transformed but not destroyed. The flood's passage had scoured some areas
while leaving others untouched, following patterns the living stone's
network had established through cooperation with my human
guidance.

Morrison returned as first light crested the eastern ridge. "No casualties," he reported with contained wonder. "Property damage limited
to uninhabited structures. Your channels directed the majority of flow
away from residential areas exactly as you predicted."

"Not predicted," Ruth corrected, appearing behind him with a
basket now completed—its spiral patterns matching exactly the living
channels that had diverted the flood. "Remembered."

"The Pentagon will have questions about tonight's operational failure," Morrison continued, federal awareness recognizing institutional
response patterns. "They'll want explanations for communication
disruption, team interception, and flood diversion that contradicts all
hydrological models."

"Let them question," Ruth replied, eight decades of resistance
teaching her that systems of power always sought explanations that
preserved their authority while dismissing phenomena that challenged
their foundations. "Some answers flow through channels their instruments can't measure."

As morning fully illuminated the valley, we walked toward the reservation center, where the community had gathered to assess the damage and coordinate its response. The blue-green plants continued their expansion, following patterns Ruth had woven throughout her lifetime, creating a living network that carried mountain memory through channels corporate extraction had tried to destroy but had inadvertently strengthened.

Along the flood's diverted paths, new growth emerged from soil once poisoned by industrial contamination. Transformation rather than destruction. Relationship rather than extraction. Memory flowing through a mountain consciousness older than human settlement.

"The Pentagon is classifying everything related to the living stone," Morrison informed us as we approached the community gathering. "Samples, research, even the blue-green plants themselves. They're implementing information containment protocols alongside physical containment strategies."

"They can classify plants and soil and water," Ruth said. "But they can't classify consciousness that flows through channels their instruments can't detect, and their models can't predict."

My blood continued its steady flow, marking the path behind us like a path leading back to the living channels that had saved reservation from the calculated flood.

"Will you testify about what happened here?" Morrison asked, considering how traditional federal procedures seek witness statements through official channels.

"We'll give your systems what they can process," I answered, recalling Ruth's words days earlier. "The rest will flow through different channels."

At the community center, elders had already organized a response with an efficiency born from generations of surviving systems designed to eliminate them. Children collected blue-green plants with instinctive recognition, their small hands guiding tendrils into patterns identical to basket designs they'd observed grandmothers weaving throughout their lives.

"They know without being taught," Ruth observed, watching the youngest generation instinctively connect with the living network. Memory carried through bloodlines the mountain recognized.

I nodded, vision shifting between physical perception and energetic awareness as radiation continued its transformation of neural pathways. "The living stone isn't just communicating with those carrying Cherokee markers," I said, watching children from other tribal backgrounds responding to plants with identical recognition. "It's establishing connections across Indigenous bloodlines, creating a network that transcends boundaries imposed by colonial systems."

Morrison watched these interactions with awe—federal training seeking categorization while human awareness recognizing arelationship beyond classification. "The Pentagon's containment strategy assumes botanical transmission limited to direct contact," he said finally. "Their models don't account for consciousness communicating across supposedly separate domains."

"Their models never do," Ruth replied simply. "That's why water always finds its original channels despite their concrete and their calculations."

As morning advanced, federal response intensified—agents establishing perimeters around the flood zone, scientists collecting samples for classified research, and communications specialists attempting to reestablish networks mountain consciousness had deliberately disrupted during the infiltration operation.

But alongside these institutional responses flowed something else —truth carried through water that remembered its original channels despite corporate rechanneling. Through plants emerging from contaminated soil in patterns identical to basket designs woven for a thousand years. Through blood connecting human consciousness to geological memory across generations.

I stood at the community's edge, watching federal containment assemble itself with institutional efficiency. Meanwhile, theliving network continued expanding through channels their instruments couldn't detect and their models couldn't predict. The radiation in my blood sang harmonies with the mountain consciousness, cellular transformation creating communication pathways that transcended individual boundaries.

"Some truths can't be classified," I whispered, watching blue-green plants respond with movement, suggesting recognition beyond botanical behavior. "Some memories can't be contained. Some relationships can't be severed."

The mountain remembered its own waterways despite corporate rechanneling, and the living stone established networks despite federal containment. The pattern hadn't just repeated but evolved—destruction became creation, extraction became relationship, and contamination became connection.

Truth rising, like water, finding its level.

Chapter Seven

THE PRISONER'S RECOGNITION

Prison orange transformed Lawrence Crowder into a different man. Not figuratively—physically.

Three months after the mound's awakening. Three months since the floodwaters receded, leaving behind toxic silt that should have rendered the valley uninhabitable for generations. Three months of blue-green growth spread through the contaminated soil in patterns identical to Cherokee basket designs. Three months of my body continuing its strange transformation—blood still flowing, but pain replaced by perception extending beyond individual boundaries.

The Metropolitan Detention Center smelled of industrial cleaner and desperation. Concrete walls painted institutional beige. Fluorescent lights buzzed at frequencies normal ears couldn't detect, but my altered hearing registered them like insect wings against glass. Through radiation-shifted senses, I could see energy signatures pulsing beneath the prison's physical structure—pipes carrying water contaminated with lead and copper, electrical wiring emitting electromagnetic frequencies that disturbed cellular communication, human bodies radiating stress hormones and diminished vitality.

Morrison stood beside me in the visitation room, his posture rigid but his eyes carrying witnessed truth no institutional reporting could fully contain. On his other side, Anita Swimmer—widow of Joseph, one of the "acceptable losses" in Crowder's cost-benefit calculation— clutched a manila folder containing photographs of the dead.

"He doesn't have to meet with us," Morrison reminded her gently. "The court ordered a psychiatric evaluation, not victim confrontation."

Anita's fingers tightened around the folder, knuckles whitening against copper skin. "I didn't come for his benefit," she said. "Or even justice. I came so he knows exactly what his quarterly profits destroyed."

The door opened with a pneumatic hiss. Two marshals escorted Lawrence Crowder into the room—the corporate titan reduced to shuffling steps in slip-on canvas shoes. The orange jumpsuit, three sizes too large, hung from shoulders that had carried tailored suits with executive authority just three months earlier. His carefully styled silver hair had been prison-cut to irregular stubble that revealed liver spots on his scalp. Without access to his personal hygienist, his skin had developed the ruddy blotchiness his corporate image consultants had spent decades concealing.

His eyes, though—those hadn't changed. Still calculating, still measuring risk against benefit, still processing human existence through a framework that reduced life to an extractable resource.

"Mr. Crowder," Morrison began with federal formality, "these individuals requested this meeting as part of their victim impact statement preparation. The judge approved limited contact under supervision."

Crowder sat with mechanical precision, hands placed flat on the metal table, expression modulated to appropriate contrition. Corporate training never fully abandoned. But something existed beneath the performance—confusion radiated from him in waves. My altered perception detected it as heat shimmeringabove summer asphalt.

"Ms. Swimmer would like to speak first," Morrison continued, then stepped back, institutional authority temporarily yielding to human grief.

Anita opened the folder with deliberate slowness. Inside lay thirty-seven photographs—not crime scene documentation but family portraits, graduation pictures, and candid moments of lives abruptly terminated by Watershed Management's flood. She spread them across the table in neat rows, creating a gallery of faces that Watershed Management's reports had reduced to statistical variables.

"Joseph Swimmer," she said, pointing to a man in his fifties with laugh lines around his eyes and a traditional ribbon shirt. "My husband. High school science teacher. Spent thirty years showing Cherokee kids they could become scientists without abandoning traditional knowledge. Drowned helping elderly neighbors evacuate."

Her finger moved to the next photograph—a teenage boy with copper hair and a basketball uniform. "Thomas Littletree. Seventeen. Had just received a full scholarship to NC State'sengineering program. Found three miles downstream caught in tree branches."

One by one, she named each person, adding details Watershed Management's risk assessments had never captured: the elder who carried five traditional stories no one else knew; the young mother who ran the community health clinic; the craftsman teaching traditional woodworking to the next generation; thetribal council member developing solar projects for reservation energy independence.

Thirty-seven names. Thirty-seven lives. Thirty-seven futures erased by corporate calculation that had deemed them "acceptable losses" against mineral extraction profits.

Crowder's expression remained carefully neutral, but his body betrayed responses corporate training couldn't fully control. Sweat beaded at his hairline. Pulse visibly throbbed at his neck. Micro-movements in facial muscles revealed a struggle between institutional conditioning and human recognition.

"Why are you showing me these?" he asked finally, voice stripped of executive resonance by three months without boardroom acoustics to amplify his authority.

"Not for your redemption," Anita replied evenly. "For their recognition. So that when you're alone in your cell tonight, you'll see faces instead of numbers. So you'll know exactly who you sacrificed for quarterly profits."

The blue-green plants I'd brought—now growing from a small clay pot on the visitation room table—responded to escalating emotional frequencies, tendrils extending toward the photographs with movement suggesting recognition beyond botanical behavior. Three months earlier, these shoots had emerged along the flood's path, drawing radiation and heavy metals from contaminated soil. Now they grew wherever I traveled, responding to my altered blood with an awareness that transcended regular plant-human interaction.

"What are those?" Crowder asked, curiosity momentarily overcoming caution as he noticed the plants' deliberate movement.

"Life returning to the soil your company poisoned," I answered, watching his eyes track the blue-green growth with fascination and alarm. "The mountain finding new channels after you tried to extract its memory."

His gaze shifted to my face, noticing for the first time the subtle changes radiation had created—the faint blue-green luminescence visible beneath my skin in patterns that exactly matched the crystalline structure of the living stone. The transformation that should have killed me but had instead created communication pathways between human consciousness and geological memory.

"You're experiencing the same cellular alteration Dr. Chen documented," he said, corporate scientist temporarily replacing executive defendant. "The molecular restructuring that began after contact with the core samples."

From the inner pocket of her jacket, Anita removed a small leather pouch. Inside lay soil collected from the flood zone—dark earth now threaded with blue-green particles visible even to unaltered perception. She placed a pinch of this soil on the table before Crowder, as deliberate as a traditional medicine carrier distributing healing herbs.

"This is what you tried to drown," she said simply.

Something in Crowder's carefully maintained façade cracked—not dramatically but fundamentally. The corporate mask slipping to reveal confusion beneath scientific certainty. "I don't understand what's happening to the valley," he admitted.

"The remediation rates defy all established models. Areas projected to remain contaminated for centuries show soil composition comparable to pre-industrial baselines after just three months. This is because your models measured separate components rather than relationship," I explained, watching blue-green tendrils respond to the soil Anita had placed before him. "Your instruments detected radiation, heavy metals, chemical compounds—but missed the living network beneath the surface."

Morrison shifted uncomfortably. What had occurred in the past three months defied conventional explanations. It failed to capture what was spreading through the valley and beyond.

"The environmental recovery rates are being studied by three different federal agencies," Morrison added, careful to remain within the boundaries his position permitted. "The results are... challenging existing remediation models."

Crowder's eyes returned to the photographs, corporate calculation temporarily yielding to human recognition. "I never personally visited the valley," he said. "These retention ponds were infrastructure features on engineering reports. These people were potential liability figures in risk assessments."

"And now?" Anita asked, the question carrying the weight of thirty-seven families still mourning their dead.

"Now I see what the abstraction concealed," he acknowledged, fingers hovering above a photograph of a child who would never reach adulthood. "The models never captured this."

The blue-green plants extended further, tendrils now forming patterns across the metal table that exactly matched the design spreading throughout the valley.

"What happens to me doesn't matter," Crowder continued, surprising us with an assessment that transcended legal strategy. "The corporate structure remains intact. The extraction imperatives continue. The board has already replaced me with someone who will implement modified versions of the same fundamental approach."

"The system persists even when individuals recognize its harm," Ruth observed, entering the room. Her silver hair was pulled back in a traditional bun, and her turquoise earrings framed aface mapped with lines of wisdom earned through resistance that outlasted extraction.

"Mrs. Nighthawk," Crowder acknowledged, recognizing the elder who had stood beside me on the mound as blue-green light revealed connections corporate science could measure but couldn't comprehend. "I didn't expect to see you here."

"The federal prosecutor needed my testimony for tomorrow's hearing," she explained, fingers working invisible river cane into patterns that matched exactly the designs the blue-green plants were forming. "I thought I'd see what corporate calculation looks like when separated from corporate power."

She set a small basket on the table—the one she'd completed the day the mound awakened, its spiral patterns matching exactly the growth now spreading through the valley. Inside lay a blue-green shoot, growing from soil collected where Crowder had stood examining core samples three months earlier.

"From the mound," she said simply.

Crowder's hand moved toward the basket with curiosity, then hesitated. "May I?"

Ruth granted him permission with a nod.

As his fingers touched the basket's rim, the plant inside responded with a subtle luminescence visible even through institutional lighting. The blue-green glow intensified, energy connecting the shoot in the basket to the growth in my clay pot and to the particles in the soil Anita had presented. Not separate elements but a unified network, communication flowing through channels corporate categorization had classified as distinct, but the living stone recognized as connected.

"It's responding to specific genetic markers," Crowder said, scientific understanding wrestling with corporate conditioning. "Establishing electrochemical communication across supposedly separate samples."

"Not just markers," I corrected, certainty flowing through altered pathways. "Relationship. Recognition between living stone's consciousness and bloodlines that have protected it for centuries."

Crowder's skepticism battled with witnessed phenomena his scientific training couldn't dismiss. "Non-organic consciousness is scientifically untenable," he insisted, institutional certainty making a final stand against direct experience.

"Yet, your instruments measured it," Ruth countered gently. "Your sensors detected what your models couldn't explain. Your equations failed because they calculated separate variables rather than fundamental relationship."

The blue-green growth continued expanding across the metal table, creating a unified network of living connections between soil samples, photographs, and human presence. Not invasive movement but deliberate communication, energy flowing through channels institutional architecture had attempted to block but couldn't fully contain.

Anita gathered the photographs with ceremonial precision, each image carefully returned to a folder that carried generations of grief that corporate calculation had attempted to transform into acceptable parameters. "The judge will determine your sentence," she said, voice steady with dignity no institutional violence could diminish. "But what happens inside you—whether you continue seeing these people as statistics or recognize them as lives with value beyond quarterly measure—that's different judgment. One you impose on yourself."

She stood to leave, Morrison moving to escort her back through institutional security. At the door, she turned one final time. "Their names matter," she said simply. "Remember them."

As they departed, Crowder's gaze returned to the blue-green growth now connecting his institutional present to mountain memory flowing through networks older than corporate structures or federal boundaries. The living stone's energy revealing a relationship that extraction had attempted to sever but had instead transformed.

"What do you want from me?" he asked finally.

"Nothing you can give through current frameworks," I answered honestly. "The system that shaped you doesn't have language for what's needed now, just as your models didn't have equations for what's growing through supposedly 'permanently contaminated' soil."

Ruth's fingers continued weaving invisible patterns that mapped memory and potential. "The mountain speaks through many voices," she said, "through Tsini's fire, through Sarah's evidence,through Esther's altered blood, through blue-green growth spreading beyond institutional containment."

"And through your recognition," I added, watching Crowder's

certainty finally crumble. "Through the gap between what your models calculated and what your human awareness now witnesses."

The marshals approached, institutional time constraints reimposing themselves on a conversation that operated through different frameworks. "This concludes today's visitation period,"the senior officer announced, federal protocols processing human interaction through administrative channels.

As Crowder stood to leave, his hand brushed the soil Anita had placed before him. Microscopic particles transferred to his fingers—blue-green growth establishing connections that would continue beyond institutional visitation limitations. Inside his cell, these particles would begin their work—transformation rather than destruction flowing through channels corporate containment couldn't fully monitor or control.

"It doesn't bring anyone back," he acknowledged as marshals prepared to escort him through security doors.

"No," Ruth confirmed, wisdom earned through eight decades of witnessing cycles of exploitation that repeated but constantly evolved. "But genuine recognition is not nothing, Mr. Crowder. There's a difference between criminals who never acknowledge the humanity of their victims and those who begin to understand what they've destroyed."

As Crowder departed, blue-green growth remained on the visitation table in patterns institutional cleaning crews would attempt to remove, but that consciousness would continue flowing through channels deeper than surface disinfection could reach—the living stone establishing a connection that transcended corporate containment and federal classification,finding paths through institutional architecture as water finds cracks in a concrete dam.

"Will he understand?" I asked Ruth as we prepared to leave, blood still flowing freely from altered pathways radiation had created between human awareness and geological memory.

"Understanding isn't a binary state," she answered. It's a process that flows through channels that many attempt to control but relationship continuously reshapes."

Outside, the morning sun illuminated a world transformed but not destroyed, damaged but not defeated, poisoned but finding healing through networks unimagined. Blue-green growth spreading across landscapes extraction had classified as permanently contaminated, following patterns Ruth had woven throughout her lifetime, carrying mountain memory through bloodlines corporate calculation had attempted to sever but had instead strengthened.

We walked toward the parking lot, where Morrison waited to drive us to the federal courthouse for tomorrow's preliminary hearing. The radiation in my blood sang harmonies with mountain consciousness, cellular transformation creating communication pathways that extended beyond individual boundaries into networks older than corporate structures or institutional boundaries.

"The legal process will continue," I acknowledged, watching thefederal system organize itself around procedures designed to balance extraction against impact. "Important channels for truth to flow through institutional architecture."

"But not the only channels," Ruth completed, basket-weaver's understanding recognizing that water follows multiple paths simultaneously. "True justice rarely flows exclusively through systems built by those who benefit from extraction."

Three months after the mound's awakening, blue-green plants continued their expansion throughout the valley and beyond—following waterways that connected supposedly separate watersheds, emerging from contaminated zones corporate models had classified as permanently damaged, establishing a living network that carried mountain memory through channels institutional containment couldn't fully monitor or control.

Inside Metropolitan Detention Center, Lawrence Crowder returned to his cell, his corporate identity transforming throughan experience no quarterly report or risk assessment had prepared him to process. The blue-green particles on his fingers began their work—microscopic threads establishing aconnection that would continue beyond institutional sentencing or corporate calculation.

Three stones. Three months. Three manifestations of a pattern that never just repeats but evolves—destruction becoming creation, extraction becoming relationship, contamination becoming connection.

The mountain remembered. And so were we.

Truth rising, like water, finding its level.

EPILOGUE: THE PATTERN EVOLVES

The birds fell silent along the eastern path.

Lily Swimmer paused on the ridge trail, copper hair catching sunlight like distant fire, her index finger raised to signal the research team behind her. Her body recognized the silence before her mind processed it—prey instinct carried in bloodlines for a thousand years.

"Wait," she whispered, eyes scanning the ridgeline where government-green Forest Service trucks had been parked yesterday. Today, sleek black SUVs occupied the same lookout points. Corporate vehicles. Private security logos barely visible on their doors. They hadn't been there at sunrise when she'd checked the trail cameras.

"What's wrong?" Professor Williams asked, consulting her GPS with an institutional dependence on technology that missed subtle truths.

"We're being watched," Lily answered, her hand instinctively touching the leather pouch at her hip where Ruth's final basket pattern was preserved—unfinished spirals drawn on deerskin with plant ink the old woman had prepared before her passing two winters ago. The same pouch contained Esther's radiation badge; its warning marker permanently black from that day at the lab ten years ago.

The university research team had been documenting the "unprecedented bioremediation phenomenon" for six months, collecting samples, publishing papers, advancing careers. What most failed to understand was that they weren't studying a phenomenon—they were participating in a conversation that had been ongoing since before Europeans arrived on the continent.

"I don't see anyone," Williams said, squinting toward the vehicles. "Probably just more government monitoring."

"Not government," Lily replied. "Private. The kind that carry guns under tailored jackets and consider ecological studies 'competitive intelligence.'" She'd learned to recognize the difference from Ruth's stories, from Esther's journals, and from the patterns that survived in the living network.

She led the team along a different path than planned, one that followed a faint line of blue-green growth nearly invisible to those who didn't know where to look. The researchers dutifully recorded GPS coordinates and collected soil samples, talking excitedly about crystal structures and remediation rates. They measured composition but missed connection. Categorized components but overlooked relationship.

"Notice how the growth follows these specific curves," Lily explained, tracing a spiral pattern identical to those in Ruth's baskets. "It's not random distribution dictated by soil chemistry. It's communication."

"Communication implies intention," Williams objected gently, her scientific framework unable to fully accommodate what her instruments measured. "Plants don't—"

"Look closer," Lily interrupted, kneeling beside a patch of blue-green shoots emerging from what had once been toxic sludge. She placed her palm flat against the crystalline growth. Within seconds, the plants visibly reoriented, turning toward her hand, edges catching the sunlight in patterns too precise to be coincidence.

The researchers murmured, adjusting equipment to document what their theoretical models couldn't explain. Lily smiled slightly. Just as Esther's journal had predicted, just as Ruth had taught her, science would eventually catch up, cataloging what traditional knowledge had always preserved.

"We should head to the collection site," Williams suggested, checking her watch. "We need those core samples before the light changes."

Lily nodded, but her attention had shifted to a flicker of movement on the ridge where the corporate vehicles were parked. Men with equipment that wasn't scientific. Long-range cameras. Soil sampling kits with company logos she recognized from economic journals—a Chinese rare earth mineral extraction firm that had recently acquired three domestic mining operations.

The pattern reasserting itself. Different players, same hunger.

"We'll take the lower path," she decided. "There's something I need to check first."

She led them down to what had once been the foundation of the Watershed Management facility. Nature had reclaimed most of the concrete—blue-green growth emerging from cracks, spreading in perfect spirals that matched Ruth's basket designs. The researchers fanned out, collecting samples, muttering about crystalline formations that shouldn't exist according to botanical taxonomy.

Lily slipped away, following a nearly invisible trail that only those with certain blood could perceive—a path marked by subtle shifts in the blue-green network's density. She reached an unmarked clearing where seven stones stood in a circle,unchanged since the gathering a decade earlier.

Kneeling at the circle's center, she removed Esther's journal from her backpack—the leather-bound notebook where her radiation-altered handwriting had recorded the beginning of her transformation. The pages contained both scientific observation and something beyond science—direct communication with theliving stone from altered consciousness.

The final entry, dated three days before Esther's physical death, read simply: I don't fear what comes. My cells have already joined the conversation that continues without my specific form. Remember: the pattern never just repeats; it evolves.

"I see them, Esther," Lily whispered, placing the journal on soil that hummed with recognition. "The same hunger, different uniforms. Just like you wrote."

She opened Ruth's pouch, removing the old woman's final basket pattern—seven spirals connected by flowing lines that anticipated exactly how the network would expand after her death. Ruth had known what was coming without satellite imagery or geological surveys. The mountain had shown her through channels corporate instruments couldn't detect.

Lily placed her palm flat against the earth where Esther's trans-formed blood had soaked into the soil seven years ago. The blue-green growth responded instantly, crystalline edges vibrating with frequencies beyond human hearing but perfectly clear to bloodlines that carried certain memories.

They're coming again, she thought into the network. Not words exactly—intention translated through neural pathways that the living stone recognized.

The response flowed back through her skin, up her arm, into consciousness that had been prepared since inception to receive such messages. Not language but understanding—images of watercourses shifting beneath corporate facilities, of crystalline growth appearing in boardrooms two thousand miles distant, of connections being established through channels no satellite could map.

We know, the network replied. We've been preparing.

Lily felt tears well—not fear or grief but recognition of beauty born from destruction. The network wasn't just cleaning toxins; it was creating resilience against future exploitation. The sacrifice of thirty-seven lives in the flood, of Sarah's determined evidence-gathering, of Esther's radiation-altered body—none had been wasted. Each had become a channel through which mountain memory now flowed.

She stood, decision crystallizing as clearly as the blue-green growth spreading beneath her feet. The research team didn't need to know about the corporate vehicles. The papers they published would record only what scientific instruments could measure, missing the deeper conversation. But she needed to warn the other tribal connections.

Returning to the researchers, she announced, "I need to leave early today. Family obligation."

Williams looked disappointed but nodded. "We can finish the collection. Will you be back tomorrow for the core samples?"

"No," Lily replied. "I'm heading to Navajo territory tonight. There's someone I need to see."

Leonard Begay's granddaughter would recognize the patterns appearing in uranium tailings near Shiprock. Together, they could strengthen the network's response before corporate extraction reached the planning stages. The same way Esther had gathered tribal repre-sentatives a decade earlier when Watershed's threat emerged.

As the team packed up the equipment and headed back toward their university vans, Lily took a different path—one that led to the exact spot where the council house had stood two centuries before, where Tsini had rescued fire from militia destruction. The blue-green growth formed a perfect circle around the site, plants standing taller and more luminescent than anywhere else in the valley.

From her pouch, Lily withdrew a clay vessel—the same one Esther had used to collect the first blue-green growth, later passed to Ruth, and finally to Lily on the old woman's deathbed. Inside, living stone fragment pulsed with quiet light that matched exactly the rhythm of Lily's heartbeat. Not just a symbolic connection but an actual biological relationship established through bloodlines that remembered what corporate extraction tried to forget.

"I'm taking you west," she told the fragment, securing the vessel in her backpack. "The network needs strengthening where new threats are gathering."

As she stood to leave, a sound made her turn—the call of a bird that shouldn't be in this forest. Not natural warning but deliberate message. Near the trail entrance stood Jamie Redhawk, his FBI credentials visible on his belt, his eyes carrying knowledge beyond institutional classification.

"I saw the vehicles on the ridge," he said without greeting. "Extraction survey team from MinShen Corporation. They've filed exploratory permits in three counties based on satellite imaging of 'anomalous remediation patterns.'"

Lily nodded, unsurprised. "The pattern never just repeats."

"It evolves," Jamie finished, the phrase carrying two decades of witnessed transformation. "Morrison sent me to warn you unofficially. The federal response is . . . bureaucratically constrained."

"As always," Lily acknowledged without bitterness, recognizingthat bureaucratic systems changed slower than corporate extraction techniques.

"What will you do?" Jamie asked.

She squared her shoulders, her copper hair catching late afternoon light in ways that painfully reminded Jamie of Esther:"What my grandmother taught me. What Esther showed us. What Ruth wove into every basket she made."

"Strengthen the network," he translated.

"The mountain remembers," Lily replied, starting down the path that would take her toward Navajo territory, the vessel secure against her back like Tsini had carried fire through flames. "And so do we."

Jamie watched her go, institutional loyalty warring with witnessed truth as it had for twenty years. Then he deliberately turned off his radio, his phone, his GPS tracker—all the technologies that connected him to systems incapable of processing the living network's response. He would delay his report by exactly twelve hours. Small resistance within federal frameworks, like water finding cracks in a concrete dam.

As Lily descended toward the valley floor, blue-green growth responded to her passing with conscious recognition. Soil that corporate extraction had calculated as permanently damaged now hummed with life that followed designs Ruth had woven into baskets six decades before Lily's birth. Water that should still carry industrial poison now ran clearer than pre-colonial testing would have shown.

Not miraculous recovery but a deliberately established relationship —the living stone's network extending through watersheds corporate boundaries had attempted to separate, creating resilience against threats already gathering beyond the horizon.

Near the valley's edge, Lily paused, turning back toward the mountains that had witnessed centuries of exploitation and resistance. The sun caught the mound's perfect curve, highlighting threads of blue-green growth that traced paths invisible to satellite imaging but clear to bloodlines that carried certain memories.

"The same pattern, different players," she whispered to the mountain, to Esther's memory flowing through living networks, to Sarah's sacrifice that had made truth visible, to Ruth's hands that had woven the future into the present. "But this time, we're ready."

She stepped onto the road, thumb extended for the ride that would connect her to other tribal lands. The clay vessel pulsed against her spine, carrying a living memory of what extraction had tried to destroy but had instead transformed. Behind her, blue-green growth continued its spiral expansion, following the final design Ruth had drawn before her death—a pattern not yet complete but already extending beyond what corporate satellites could track.

The mountain had remembered. The water had carried what

corporate calculation tried to drown. The pattern continued—not just repeating but evolving, creating a response to exploitation that didn't just resist but transformed.

Truth rising, like water, finding its level.

Not ending, but becoming.

The End

Check out genescottbooks.com for novels, photographs, essays, and book club reading guides!